HEAVEN'S MOST WANTED

HER ANGELS BOOK 3

ERIN BEDFORD

ALSO BY ERIN BEDFORD

Academy of Witches

Witching on a Star

As You Witch

Witch You Were Here

The Underground

Chasing Rabbits

Chasing Cats

Chasing Princes

Chasing Shadows

Chasing Hearts

Fairy Tale Bad Boys

Hunter

Pirate

Thief

Mirror

Stepbrother

The Celestial War Chronicles

Song of Blood and Fire

Visions of War and Water

The Mary Wiles Chronicles

Marked By Hell

Bound By Hell

Deceived By Hell

Tempted By Hell

The Crimson Fold

Until Midnight

Vampire CEO

Granting Her Wish

"Are you sure this is what whipped cream is meant for?" Gabriel asked, holding the spray can in his hand.

We were in the back room of the Gotcha! Offices where we'd been taking our lunch break. And by lunch, I meant that I was showing Gabriel that food was not just for eating but also for other recreational needs. We'd already gone through the chocolate sauce which I had happily lapped off Gabriel's very lickable abs. Now it was onto the whipped cream. I only regret not having cherries to top it all off.

I propped myself up on the table by my elbows and nodded. "Oh, yeah," my voice came out raspy, a bit breathless from my last orgasm, and I took a moment to swallow and lick my lips. "Definitely."

"It doesn't say so on the can." Gabriel's green eyes sparkled as he shook the can at me. It really wasn't fair. Sure, he was an angel, but guys just shouldn't look that good. His light brown hair fell over his eyes, and trust me, it felt a good as it looked. Pair that with dimples that made my knees weak, and that mouth... God, that mouth. Lucifer gave the best oral, but I had to admit Gabriel was quickly becoming neck and neck with the devil.

I returned his lopsided smile with a quirk of my brow. "Sure, it does. Right there on the side." I gestured with my head toward the can as I grabbed the washcloth off the table where I was laid out, naked from the waist down.

Gabriel snorted, his eyes on the can's label. "You mean the part that says, 'Refrigerate after opening?'"

Hopping off the table, I snatched the can out of his hand and shoved it back into the mini fridge. "Yeah, after opening. Nowhere does it say what it has to be used for." I turned back around only to find myself caged between the counter and Gabriel's massive arms. Tipping my head back, I grinned up at him. "My ass is getting cold."

"Well, let me remedy that for you." Gabriel's hands slid down to my ass, cupping each cheek and pulling me close. Just when I thought I might be getting another orgasm before one o'clock, the chime on the front door went off.

"Ignore him," Gabriel muttered as his fingers dipped between my thighs to play with my folds.

My knees stuttered and a small moan escaped from my closed lips. I gasped, my head falling back his fingertip circled my clit. Rocking against his hand, my fingers curled around his biceps, but I neither pushed away nor pulled him closer as he thoroughly distracted me from whoever was waiting on the other side of the thin wall.

I felt more than saw the quirk of Gabriel's lips against the side of my face when I parted my legs further for him. My fingers fumbled with the zipper of his pants, desperate to touch him the way he was touching me, and I almost had him when a masculine voice called out, "Hello? Is anyone here?"

My hand stilled. Eyes fluttering open, I licked my lips and took in a few deep breaths to calm my racing heart. Gabriel wasn't having any of it though. He pressed himself into my hand trying to bring me back to the moment.

Pulling back, I frowned at Gabriel. "Did you see him coming?"

Avoiding my gaze, Gabriel flicked my clit with his thumb which made me gasp before he scowled. That answered that question. He had. For an angel, sometimes he was low down rotten, especially when it came to me.

However, as much as I wanted to continue our competition to see who could make the other cum more, I had a job to do. I couldn't let my good name go in the dirt because I was too busy playing hide the pickle.

"Hello?" the voice called out once more even closer now.

"Hold on a moment," I called back, giving Gabriel a look before pushing him back from me. I grabbed my discarded skirt, pulled it back on, then shoved my feet into my flip flops before spinning around on the smirking angel. "Where're my panties?"

Giving me a cocky grin, Gabriel leaned against the counter, his arms crossed over his bare chest he had yet to cover. "I don't know. Maybe you left them..."

"Uh, madam?" the voice from before rose with

a bit of laughter in it. "I believe you might have lost something."

"Shit," I hissed under my breath, glaring at a far too amused Gabriel on my way out of the back room. My hands rushed to my head, smoothing and pulling as I tried to fix my hair which I was sure looked like a rat's nest had an orgy in it. When I was satisfied it was the best it was going to get, I put on my best professional smile and rounded the corner.

"Hello, welcome to Gotcha! I'm Jane, your resident psychic detective. How can I he… help… guh… you?" I gagged on my words as I caught sight of the boyishly handsome man holding my hot pink thong between his fingertips.

Standing at six foot two, he had loose blonde curls cut to brush his ears, big blue eyes, and a smile that would make even a straight man turn. He was like one of those naked baby cherubs you found on a cathedral's ceiling, you know, if he had grown up into a massive hunk of man meat.

Damn.

"Are these yours?" He offered me the thong which was hanging by a string on his fingertip.

"Uh…" I trailed off, half mortified and half stunned by the man in front of me. I was jolted out of my brain fart when a hand clamped down on my shoulder.

Gabriel stood behind me, still shirtless, the show-off, and held a hand out to the stranger. "Thanks, I'll take those." The arrogance in his voice was unusual for the usually carefree archangel. I gaped up at him as the stranger tossed him my panties with an arched brow. Gabriel caught them and tucked them into his pocket before leaning over and kissing me on the side of the head. "I've got to go, see you later."

Still barefoot and shirtless, Gabriel marched out of the office with a bit more swagger than usual in his step. I blinked, my mouth opening and closing like a fish. What the hell had just happened? And where the hell did Gabriel think he was going like that?

The archangel couldn't be corporeal without me, well, my blood more specifically, so him having anywhere to be while he had a good hour or so before he faded out of everyone's view but my own was a mystery. Not to mention he was still half dressed. A part of me wanted to chase him down and make him put some damn clothes on. He was mine to ogle, God damn it. I put a lot of miles into that angel, and I wasn't about to let some Botoxinjected floozy on the strip where my shop sat fondle what was mine.

While I was having a good little hissy fit, the stranger cleared his throat, and I clamped my mouth shut. Giving my head a bit of a shake, I turned back to the gorgeous man. "I'm sorry about that, how can I help you?"

His lips curling into an amused grin, the man, who I now noticed was dressed in an expensive three-piece suit, offered me his hand. Rolex, nice. "Let's start over. I am Andre Belmont. And you are...?"

God, even his name was sexy. Andre Belmont. I bet it felt good to say out loud. It just screamed mouth orgasm. Maybe Mandy could use a pick me up? I hadn't seen my bestie with anyone recently. I'd have shamelessly flirted with him if I wasn't already involved with three angels. Three very possessive and domineering angels who would eat a guy like him for breakfast. Wait, did angels eat breakfast in heaven? I'd have to ask them.

Nutritional needs aside, I couldn't have the man in front of me, so I might as well give him to my bestie. Besides, who could outdo an angel? That's right. No one.

Putting the thought away for later, I held out my hand. "Jane Mehr. A pleasure to meet you."

To my surprise, he didn't shake my hand but turned it over and brushed his warm lips across the top of my knuckles. "The pleasure is mine, of course."

Taking my hand back with a nervous chuckle, I resisted the urge to wipe it off where the tingles still lingered. He's for Mandy. For Mandy.

"Uh, so." I clapped my hands together, fidgeting in place. "What can I help you with? Lost dog? Cheating spouse? Perhaps, a missing item of substantial value?"

His baby blue eyes widened slightly. "You really are as good as they say. I have recently lost a trophy made of pure solid gold. It's supposed to be awarded to the winner of my contest next week."

Ha. One point to Jane. I didn't even need the angels for this one, though naming off all the normal things rich people come to see me for hardly counted as being psychic. This guy was just easy to please it seemed.

Hopefully, the case would be just as easy to solve.

I hummed and moved over to my desk, pulling out a note pad to take notes. Gesturing a hand toward the chair in front of me, I said, "Take a seat."

Andre, God, that name, crossed over to my desk in two long strides and sat down as if he were liquid in human form, pouring himself into the seat. Lucifer would be jealous of this guy's suaveness.

"So, how about we start at the beginning?" I told him, staring down at my paper so as not to stare at him too long. "You say you lost a golden trophy? And by lost, you mean stolen?"

It wasn't a hard leap. No one just loses a trophy. Well, okay, so I have been known to lose things like that all the time, but normal people? Not likely. Hence someone had to have stolen it. Besides, why would they come to me if they had accidentally left it in their canary yellow Ferrari?

Andre shifted in his seat, his eyes darting around the room as he cleared his throat. He clearly did not like the subject I had brought up. "Yes, stolen. We keep it in a safe. It was there last Friday, but now, it's gone."

Okay. We had a timeline. Between Friday and today, Monday, their golden trophy was in a safe. Approximate time it was stolen? Within 72 hours.

"And why haven't you filed this with the police?" I looked up from my paper and focused on his nose.

That was safe, right? It was just a nose. A perfectly shaped nose. One that would feel like Heaven sliding down my...

"Miss Mehr?"

Blinking rapidly, I placed my hands down on the counter and shook my head. "Sorry, I lost my focus for a moment." I gave him a silly grin accompanied by a nervous chuckle. "You know, visions. Never know when they are going to pop up." Fucking Christ, he's for Mandy, not me. I should have let Gabriel finish me off before he left. All this left-over sexual tension was making my hormones go wacky.

Andre's perfectly pouty lips pressed together in half concern and the other half curiosity. "Do you have visions often?"

"Oh, yeah." I waved him off, crossing one leg over the other. My knee hit the underside of my desk, and I winced. I tried to save face by saying, "Happens all the time."

"And what did you see?" He leaned forward, his eyes intently focusing on me like was trying to see into my head. "Anything about my trophy?"

"Uh, no, not yet. Sorry. Sometimes the images are a bit fuzzy at first. I am getting something gold and shiny," I bullshitted to him as the eagerness in his eyes only grew. "Anyway, you were telling me why you didn't go to the police for this matter? Most don't come to me until they have no other options."

Andre sighed and rubbed a large hand over his face. "Police only complicate matters. If I tell the police, then it will be leaked to the press, and there would be a huge scandal. It would just ruin my reputation. No one would trust me to run the competition again."

That made sense. There were plenty of rich folks who came to me because they wanted to keep their issues on the down low. Like that pool boy who videotaped himself fucking the Mayor's son, quite enthusiastically I might add. Hey, my job had to have some perks. While the free porn had been great, it had also been thrilling to hunt down the tape and all its copies as well as put the fear of God, or Archangel, into him so that he'd never do anything like it again.

God, I loved my job.

"So, what kind of competition do you run?" I moved my eyes over him, purely professionally, trying to decipher something to tip me off on what kind of work he does.

"Well, isn't it obvious?" Andre held his hands

out to the side as if I should be able to tell from his body. Believe me, I was looking really hard. When I only stared at him, he huffed. "Fashion. I run a fashion competition. Hundreds of aspiring fashion designers from all over the country come and compete for the Belmont Award. It's been in my family for years. Except this year, I've blown it."

Fashion, huh? I would never have pegged it. I mean, he dressed nice enough, but I only knew enough about clothes to tell he liked expensive things. Sadly, his profession made me question if he would even like Mandy's… equipment. He might bat for the other team.

Only one way to find out.

"Oh, don't think that way. I'm sure you did everything you could to keep the trophy safe," I cooed, placing a hand on the desk reaching toward him. I let my shirt tug down so that my cleavage was bare to his gaze. If he were gay, he wouldn't look, right? "Things happen, but I'm sure I can help you get your trophy back without anyone being the wiser." I squeezed my arms against the sides of my breasts, really giving the girls a good push up.

And there it was. His eyes flicked down to my chest, and a slight heat slid across his gaze as his tongue darted out to wet his mouth. When his eyes moved back to mine, desire was clearly there in his dilated pupils. Bingo.

"Are you sure?" His voice took on a raspy, lower tone that made me wiggle in my seat. Mandy was a lucky girl, she just didn't know it yet.

I stood and gave him a megawatt smile. "Positive."

He let out a large breath and placed a hand on his chest. "You don't know how much of a relief that is." Andre stood, his height towering over me.

I tried my eyes to stay north of the border, but I couldn't help but notice the tent in his pants that had not been there before. Mandy was a very lucky girl. I dragged my eyes back to his face, forcing myself to pay attention to what he was saying.

"The trophy has been a hallmark of my family's legacy. I mean, besides the cash prize, a hundred thousand dollars."

My eyes bugged out of my head. A hundred thousand dollars? To design some clothes? I was not in the right industry.

Forcing my eyes back into my head, I offered him my best reassuring smile as I came around my desk. "Mr. Belmont, I will do my utmost to preserve your family's legacy. You can count on me." I patted his chest without thinking.

"Call me Andre. And that's good. I'm happy to hear it." His eyes dipped down, the distance between us smaller than I had intended. If he got any closer, that python in his pants was going to be right up against me.

Putting a polite but closed off smile on my face, I took a step back from him and dropped my arm. "Uh, so this is my retainer fee, plus my hourly amount." I pushed my usual contract across the table. "Of course, I will need to be able to bill you for essentials, whatever I need to blend into your competition."

"Blend in?" He cocked his head to the side. "You can't figure out who did it from here?"

I laughed. "No, Andre. I'm good but not that good." I shifted some papers and didn't meet his eyes. "I'll need to mingle with your crew and the contestants, get a feel for their auras. See if I can pick up any lingering emotions or at least get a premonition, you know?"

"Ah, of course. Whatever you need." He took the contract and without reading it signed on the dotted line. "There, when can you start? Can you come now?"

My mind immediately went into the gutter. Stop it. Gabriel hadn't even been gone for half an hour, and already I wanted to jump the nearest guy. I was getting spoiled by all these hot guys giving me orgasms at the drop of a hat.

Glancing around for any of my usual company, I pushed a thought out. *I need a little help here. Someone, anyone. Help.* When no one appeared and it was getting awkward just sitting there, I gave up.

Grabbing my purse, I nodded towards the door. "I'm all yours."

2

Following Andre out of my office, I had a good feeling about this. I'd had an array of cases since I opened Gotcha! several weeks ago but none so exciting as this one.

A fashion designer contest. Man, Mandy was going to freak out when she heard. I held back a little squeal of delight. Be professional, Jane. Don't let the hot...

My thoughts trailed off as my eyes landed on two men standing across the street. Normally, random people standing around chitchatting wouldn't bother me. However, these two were other worldly attractive and they were looking at me. They weren't being very sneaky about it.

Angels. Great.

I knew they'd come for me eventually. It was only a matter of time. Uriel had given too many warnings to have them never show up.

Trying not to let them know, that I know they were watching me, I turned my attention back to the man with me and his... limo waiting for us. Fucking hell.

"What is it you do again, Mr. Belmont?" I casually asked, my head tilting to the side to get a better look at him.

"Please, Andre." He reminded me again as he let the chauffeur open the door for us. We both slid inside the limo, and I almost peed my pants in excitement.

I hadn't been in a limo since... well ever. Sleek black leather seats covered every wall but the doors and a black box. When Andre opened it and pulled out a bottle of water, I about had a heart attack. The limo was big enough to freaking live in and had a mini-fridge to boot.

Okay, so it didn't have a toilet, but I could pee outside. Not like I haven't done it before.

Before I could reminisce more about my outdoor adventures, I took the water from him and leaned back in my seat. "So, your job?"

Andre sat beside me, not so far away that it was weird but close enough that I could feel his body heat. "Well, it's a bit hard to explain. It's certainly nothing as exciting at solving crimes or being a psychic."

"It's not that exciting, though I do like being my own boss." For the most part, I giggled to myself thinking about my demanding angels and took a drink from the water bottle as my eyes shifted to the window. The limo had started to move, and the world passed by at a glacial pace. Traffic in this part of town was brutal, I'd be surprised if we made it anywhere within the hour. Good thing I had the rest of the day clear.

Andre's eyes crinkled at the corners, clearly amused by my answer before he continued to explain. "I own several clothing franchises which requires me to vet out the next big thing. It's all very drab when you think about it. Lots of numbers and calculations. I have to factor in the risks and rewards of taking on a new line. However, it has made me quite rich, so I can hardly complain."

He said it all so nonchalantly that it was a bit hard to believe. However, I wasn't the type to have more than a few dimes to rub together, so maybe once you have so much money you don't know what to do with, it becomes obsolete. I certainly wouldn't mind it.

I hummed to show him I was interested and tilted my lips up slightly. So, he was in the billion-aire range. At least, I didn't have to worry about him not being able to foot the bill. I took another drink of my water and was about to ask him another question when a large blonde Adonis appeared on the other side of the limo, one long leg crossed over the other an annoyed look in his hyper-observant gaze.

Water caught in my throat and I covered my mouth, coughing repeatedly.

It was Michael.

"Are you alright?" Andre asked as he came over to me, his large hand patting my back.

I waved him off, my eyes watering and lungs burning. "Yes. Sorry. Wrong pipe."

Forcing my eyes to stay on Andre even though I could see Michael out of the corner of my eye, I asked, "So, picking clothes? That sounds interesting. I have a hard enough time figuring out what I like, let alone what the rest of the world wants."

Michael snorted and shook his head slightly. Pieces of his hair fell over his eyes, eyes that smoldered with dominance and impatience. He wanted me to pay attention to him.

Well, he would just have to wait.

Concern still on his face, Andre gave me a short nod. "It can be challenging. However..." His voice trailed off for a moment, the corner of his lip quirking up. "I don't think hot pink thongs will ever go out of style."

Flushing deeply, I ducked my head and turned my face away from him. "Uh, yeah. Sorry about that."

I could see Michael's brows shoot up to his hairline, his blue eyes quizzical. His eyes on me made me shift in my seat, and I felt like I should explain what Andre was talking about, but the billionaire beat me to it.

"Was that man your… boyfriend?" The subtlety to the way he asked almost made me smile, but then I reminded myself this one was for Mandy. I had enough dicks on my hands already… figuratively speaking… and one of them was already there staring holes into Andre like the angel wanted to smite the man on the spot.

I gave Michael a warning look before I glanced back to Andre. "Uh, yeah. Gabriel. I guess you could call him my boyfriend."

Michael made an amused sound, and I resisted the urge to look at him. I couldn't talk to invisible angels in front of clients. It tended to put a damper on their confidence in me.

"He seemed very protective of you," Andre continued, not knowing we had an eavesdropper. His brows crinkled and his head jerked slightly. "And bold. Was he aware he was only half dressed when he left?"

I laughed and waved a hand in the air. "Oh, yeah. That's Gabriel. He's a bit of a free spirit. One of those guys who'd rather feel the ground beneath his feet."

Andre nodded as if he understood. If only he knew.

Letting out a relieved breath, I chanced a peek at Michael. Dressed in a dark blue sweater with a white strip across the chest, he had one long leg crossed over the other. His black slacks inched up at the ankle, showing he had once again decided to forgo socks with his loathers.

Speaking of a weird fashion sense.

"You let this human see your underwear?" Michael asked. His voice filled the limo to make it substantially smaller.

Staring him down, I didn't answer him. He knew I couldn't… or wouldn't, anyway. Thankfully, I didn't have to pretend not to see or hear him for very long before the limo stopped, and the door opened on Andre's side first.

As soon as he was out, I shot my eyes to Michael and muttered, "Ask Gabriel. I'm working."

"I can see that." The condescending tone in Michael's voice really grated my nerves.

I flipped him off and climbed out of the car, taking the hand Andre offered me. We walked across the parking lot of the large building they used for basketball games and concerts. I actually remembered seeing some kind of advertisement for this contest now that we were here. When we entered the building, Michael appeared next to us, not at all deterred by my rude gesture.

"I already spoke to Gabriel," he intoned seriously. "He had other business to attend to and asked me to take his place since your new client made your arousal spike and you are currently pantiless."

I made a strangled sound in my throat which caused Andre to give me a concerned look. "Uh, do you have a bathroom?"

"Oh, yes. Down there to the right." Andre

pointed to one side of the entrance area. "I'll wait for you."

Nodding, I quickly made my way to the bathroom with Michael hot on my heels.

Once inside the bathroom, I checked the stalls and thankfully found them empty. Spinning around, I locked the door and then pointed an accusatory finger at Michael.

"What the hell?" I whispered harshly. "I'm with a client. Don't bring up personal shit while I'm not somewhere I can talk to you about it. Even more so when you are in-fucking-visible!"

Michael's eyes narrowed, and the air in the bathroom thickened. He never did tell me how he did that. The archangel was incorporeal for the most part but could still affect the air around him. So much so that when he got upset, he could shake the whole building.

Hoping I wasn't about to have to listen to the Hand of God have a hissy fit, I crossed my arms over my chest and tapped my foot. "Well, out with it. We're alone now."

Marching over to where I stood, Michael came so close that had he been corporeal I'd have been able to feel his breath on my face. "You forget yourself, Jane. We are doing everything in our power to keep you safe and away from those who would take advantage of your delightful nuisances. Uriel is throwing a fit all over heaven because we even come down here to see you, and yet here you are, complaining because I'm doing my job."

"So, I'm just a job to you?" I couldn't help the hurt in my voice. I know, I know. I'm a fucking hypocrite. I bitch that he's here and then bitch because he's not here for the right reasons.

Michael's face softened. "Of course not. You know that, and you also know that while the others and I willingly share you with each other. That doesn't mean we want to share you with that human man."

My heart melted a bit. Big tough warrior angel was jealous. If I didn't know it would hurt his fragile ego, I'd poke fun at Michael right now. Instead, I went for denial.

Hands on my hips, I tossed my head in a dramatic huff. "What makes you think I want to have sex with Andre?"

Cocking a knowing brow at me, Michael's fingers moved along the front of my body which caused it to buzz pleasantly. "Besides the obvious sting of your arousal, Gabriel said you were… what was that word he called it?" He glanced to the side for a moment, his fingertips stilling before they touched my more aware spots. With a grunt and a steely gaze, Michael growled, "… drooling."

I scoffed. "Uh. No. I was not drooling. So, Andre is… he's relatively attractive," I ended lamely, then quickly added, "But I was not drooling."

Eyes still locked on mine, Michael withdrew a familiar pair of panties. Geez, those were getting around. "So, you didn't allow that human to touch these? Or leave with him while bare beneath that skirt?"

"Not on purpose and…" I frowned and then made a grab for the panties my hand falling through the material. "Just give them back."

This time Michael's lips curled into a wicked grin. "Give me your blood, and I'd be happy to."

Normally, I'd be all over that. A little cut, Michael gets to be solid for an incalculable amount of time. Today, though, I knew if I gave him the chance to touch me, he'd make me pay. He wasn't the right hand of God for nothing.

Michael liked being in control. He also liked a bit of pain with his pleasure, even more so if he were doing it somewhere I wouldn't normally allow it. The bathroom of a public building with a client waiting for me just outside the door? Oh, yeah. It was right up his alley.

I glanced between the panties and the angel and debated on whether it was worth it.

I'd gone commando before. It wasn't something new to me, but the dare in Michael's eyes annoyed me. Like he knew I wouldn't do it and it pleased him to no uncertain measure to know he had me at his mercy.

Well, we'd have to see about that.

"Fine," I snipped, pulling the safety pin from the bottom of my shirt I kept for occasions like this. Unhooking the sharp end, I pricked my finger with barely a wince, I was so used to it. I should just invest in some diabetic finger pokers. Probably way more sterile.

The blood had just touched the surface when Michael's head dipped. His mouth wrapped around my finger, and the buzzing turned into the feeling of his warm wet mouth sucking on my finger. I'd be lying if every slide of his tongue, every tug of his mouth against my digit didn't zip straight to my groin.

Fuck me.

Michael's hand latched onto my wrist, and he backed me up until I was pressed against the sink. His long lashes flipped up, those blue eyes stormy and full of promises that made me shiver. His mouth gave my finger one more long tug before he released it.

My breathing came faster now. All thoughts of why I'd been arguing with him out the door ended as he picked me up and sat me on the counter. His mouth clashed with mine, and my arm around his neck pulled him closer, my legs wrapping around his waist. I sighed into his mouth and let myself forget everything but him.

We rarely got these moments anymore. Half the time before we were even able to get anything started, one or all the guys were called away for something which was why I when I had the chance, I had taken advantage of Gabriel at the office.

A woman had needs, God damn it.

Thinking of earlier made me realize I'd forgotten about my panties still in Michael's hand, now very much corporeal.

Withdrawing my mouth with much reluctance, I gasped, "Michael. I have a client waiting."

He ignored me. His hand cupped my face, then

arched my neck so he could trail his mouth down the length of it. For a moment, I forgot what I was saying as his mouth found a particularly sensitive spot behind my ear. Then my eyes landed on the pink material in the hand touching my face.

I reached for it.

Then the hand was gone.

No longer touching my face, I had only a second to wonder where it went before I cried out. Michael's thumb pressed down on my clit, rubbing it in little circles. It felt different though, as if something was between his hand and my skin.

My eyes snapped open as they locked onto Michael's smirking face. "You're going to... ah... stop that."

"You know that's not how this works, Jane." Michael rumbled against me, his lips nipping at my ear as his hand drove me to the brink of insanity.

I could have made him stop. He would have if I had really meant it. We both knew I didn't though, or I'd have pushed him away. Instead of worrying that my client was waiting just outside or that we were in a public restroom, I spread my legs wider for him allowing him to take exactly what he wanted, what both of us wanted.

Of course, like the bastard he was, the moment I gave in, Michael stopped. Before I could say, "Bob's your uncle," my panties were back on and Michael was three feet away from me, unlocking the door and ducking out.

I gaped at where he had once stood, not quite believing what had just happened. Then after a second, I scrunched my face up and dropped from the counter to adjust my ruffled clothing. "That son of a bitch."

"Miss Mehr?"

Startled by Andre's voice, I cleared my throat and smoothed one more hand down my hair before pulling the bathroom door open. I wasn't sure how much more my poor body could take of this torture. My hair was certainly suffering.

Still throbbing and wet from Michael's ministrations, I offered Andre an apologetic smile. "Sorry about that."

"Not a problem," Andre answered. "I stepped away for a moment to answer a question and thought I might have missed you."

"Nope. I'm right here." On the fucking edge because my angel boyfriend wouldn't let me cum, who was also conveniently missing in action. Where the hell did he go?

"Well, then shall we?" Andre waved a hand toward the entrance. As we walked into the massive center, Andre continued to tell me about the theft. "So, as you can see the area is pretty open. There isn't much security right now because the convention has started yet. There is just the guard who checks for your badge."

I hadn't noticed that guard when we were on the way in but then again, my concerns were on the looming archangel. I quickly scanned the room looking for that Viking-sized angel but couldn't see him in the throngs of gorgeous models running to and fro as they got fitted and prodded for the contest.

There were booths set up for each designer where they had curtains around the majority of their areas but had a few pieces sitting out on their table. No doubt the designers wanted to hide from the competition but still wanted to shove their talent in their faces.

"Where did you keep the trophy?" I asked, keeping my voice low so as to not bring attention to us. If Andre didn't want the police involved because of the press, then he definitely didn't want the contestants to know.

"This way." Andre placed a hand on my lower

back quite a bit lower than what was polite. He directed me toward a set of offices. Before we left the main area, Michael, surprise, surprise, popped out of nowhere and headed us off. Andre jerked to a stop, confusion marring his face but then noticed Michael staring at me. "Another boyfriend of yours?"

I offered him an apologetic smile. "Something like that. I asked Michael to meet me here. He helps with the psychic process."

Andre hummed. I wasn't sure if he believed me, but he didn't press. Instead, he dropped his hand from my back and took a step away. At least, he wasn't stupid. "The safe is in here."

Behind Andre's back, Michael's lip ticked up at one side, and one of his perfect brows arched. I glared at him and pinched his thick muscular arm.

"Was that supposed to hurt?" he asked.

"I'm going to show you pain when I get home," I muttered under my breath so low only he could hear with his heightened senses. "You're going to feel my foot so far up your ass, you'll be begging to get me—"

"Did you say something?" Andre turned from the door where he had just unlocked it.

Lacing my fingers behind my back, I beamed at him. "Just thinking out loud. Don't mind me."

"Alright," Andre drew out and then ushered us inside.

Michael and I entered the office behind him. I could already see Michael searching the room for clues as Andre pointed out the safe. One of Michael's specialties was being hyper-aware of everything. He could find a needle in a haystack from a mile away. It made finding details humans otherwise wouldn't notice far easier.

"This is the Mortenson 5000." Andre stopped next to the safe and tapped a hand on top of it with a proud gleam in his eyes.

I watched him nodding as if I knew what the hell he was talking about, but to me, it was a safe. Black and big as the mini fridge in the limo, it stood on a table in the back of the office where anyone could see it. That's about the most I knew about safes, so not much really.

Andre put in the code and opened the door, showing the empty inside. "We keep the trophy here. Or we did. Now, it's just for looks." He sighed, a pained expression on his face. "This was supposed to be uncrackable. For the pretty penny I spent on it, I'd hoped for at least some kind of dynamite needed to open it without the code."

He shrugged, rubbing a hand over his mouth. "Alas, it is what it is." He turned those sad eyes toward me, a pleading expression on his face. "Please tell me you can find it. I don't have time to commission another one before the event starts."

It wasn't even about the money it cost. Just that he didn't have time to make a new one. Well, at least, that was something I could check off my list. He didn't steal his own trophy to get the insurance money from it, and they always had insurance on things like this.

Giving him a sympathetic smile, I moved toward him, prepared to reassure him, but Michael stepped in front of me. He crossed his arms over his chest and tried to use his size to intimidate Andre. Unfortunately for him, Andre wasn't easily intimidated. Though two inches shorter than Michael, he didn't let having to look up at the Archangel bother him.

"Trust us, we will find your trophy. Then you can go back to your little contest." Michael's usual condescension filled his voice, and I feared he was going to get me fired before I even got my retainer fee.

Andre didn't even blink. He pulled his phone from his pocket and typed in a few words before turning his gaze to me. "My accountant has wired the retainer fee to your account. I assume that means you can start today?"

Gaping at how quick he was about it, I nodded dumbly. "Uh, yeah. Sure. Let's go."

ndre led Michael and me out of the office and back into the main arena. With an over-exaggerated sweep of his hand, he gestured for us to head into the thick of things.

"So, what's the plan? How are you going to introduce me?" I asked, my eyes catching onto every stall as we passed by. There were so many models of all shapes and sizes here, way different from anything I had ever seen on television.

Wrapping an arm around my shoulders, Andre leaned his head down to mine so he could whisper, "We could go a few different ways with this. You could be my latest female companion…?" He gave me a knowing look, but I wasn't quite getting what he meant.

"Female companion?" I arched a brow but then let out an eep when Michael's arm wrapped around my waist and jerked me to his side. Glaring up at the mountain of a man, I gaped, "What was that for?"

"He means to have you act as his lover," Michael growled, his eyes narrowed and locked onto Andre. The possessive hold he had on my waist was not at all unwelcome.

"Oh... oh!" I glanced between the two of them. "Uh, yeah that probably isn't a good idea. How about something else? Maybe something along the lines of I'm an up-and-coming business woman looking to get into the fashion field?" I offered with an encouraging smile.

Andre's brows pinched together, but he conceded with a sigh. "Oh, very well. My idea would have been more fun, but you're the psychic. You know what's best."

"That I do." I grinned as I lifted a finger up and waved it in the air. "Now," I clapped my hands together with glee, "where should we start?"

"This way." Andre reached out to place a hand on my back but dropped it at the warning grunt that Michael released. "We'll start at hair and makeup."

"Oooh!" My lips spread out into a gleeful grin as I eagerly followed after Andre. I wasn't giving Michael too much attention. While I enjoyed his alpha male actions, letting him know that would only urge him to do it more. Then I'd have three archangels fighting over who got to throw me over their shoulders and drag me back to their cloud for some bang-bang.

Actually, on second thought…

"Lisa, Marco," Andre called out to one of the booths, and two people turned around.

"Yo, boss man. What's up?" A short woman snapped her bubble gum in our direction then chomped at it with her mouth wide open. Her pixie cut hair swooped up in a mixture of blue and pink streaks. Big earrings decorated her ears and almost brushed the shoulders of the jersey dress covering her petite form.

"This is Jane." Andre gestured toward me, not at all disturbed by the way Lisa addressed him. "She's interested in learning the finer points of fashion, and I thought it would be a nice treat for her to see what the models have to undergo before hitting the runway."

Lisa's eyes immediately went to me, scanning me up and down as if she were assessing my value. The other person who had to be Marco, a large bald guy of Latino heritage who had more muscles than a pro-wrestler, glanced over me with brief interest and then went back to digging into his makeup box.

"Aight, I guess we could give the lady the whole workaround," Lisa said before glancing to Marco. "You in, Marco? Think you can handle the face work while I attack that crow's nest?"

Lisa's words made me reach for my hair with a frown. I didn't know what she was talking about I'd brushed my hair today. Sure, I hadn't gotten around to getting it professionally done lately, but still, it was a bit harsh.

"Jane?" Andre arched a brow as if silently asking if I was ready.

A bit nervous about being left alone in a place so out of my element, I gave him a nervous smile and a thumbs up before taking the seat Lisa patted for me to take. Michael stood off to the side, his arms crossed over his chest, while he kept an eye on the surroundings. He didn't seem much at all worried about what they were about to do to me.

"Good!" Andre pulled his phone out of his

pocket and tapped a few things into it. "I'll be back to check on you after a while. Please, feel free to look around and remember… have fun." He winked and grinned at me before stalking away.

"Ooo, that man is fine." Lisa hissed out, waving a long-nailed hand at her face and smacking her gum once more. "So, what's the deal with this one?" Her dark eyes moved between Michael and me.

I opened my mouth to answer, but Michael beat me to it. "I am Michael, the Hand of God and protector of this mortal woman. All those who dare to cause her harm will face my wrath."

While Lisa and Marco gaped at Michael, I facepalmed but couldn't help but grin like a silly school girl. Really, who could say that they had the Archangel Michael willing to bring down the all mighty wrath of Heaven on their behalf? No one but me, that's who.

"Woohoo. Man, you are lucky, gurrrl." Lisa waved her comb in Michael's direction with a smirk. "I wish my man was that dedicated. Right now, I can barely get him to text me back. Am I right, Marco?"

"That pendón doesn't know what he's got." Marco clucked his tongue and picked up a couple bottles of foundation before holding them up to my face. "Hermosa, you are more blanco than my jockey shorts."

I flushed and giggled. "Well, what can I say? The sun hates me."

The two of them chitchatted around me while they applied makeup here and pulled my hair there. While I enjoyed the pampering, it was a bit too much. I'd be happy to be done and see the final product. Michael stood by with his arms crossed over his chest, his eyes taking in everything around us, not missing a single thing.

"So…" I started after a bit. "Do you do the makeup and hair for all the models?"

Lisa shook her head. "Nah, there are at least half a dozen of us. There are far too many for just the two of us. We usually only handle Kesha and Jean Claude's people. It would be three, but Chloe…"

"Shush, mama. Do you wanna get fired?" Marco shot Lisa a warning look. "We can't be losing a good gig like this for being a chismoso."

"What?" I asked, glancing between the two with more interest now. "What's a ch… chismomoso?"

Marco paused mid-swipe of his eye brush. "Chismoso. A gossip. That's one thing you need to learn about this business, hermosa. You keep your lips shut and your eyes open."

Lisa nodded fervently. "These people are big on keeping your mouth shut. Nobody wants their ideas ripped off, and that's the best way to get yourself blacklisted."

"Oh, I get it." I nodded. "Snitches get stitches or whatnot."

"Exactly, but in this case, you won't work anywhere in the state or, in some cases, the whole country if they find out you be flapping your jab." Lisa shoved some clips into her apron and then pulled out her hair spray. "Hold yer breath, girly. This stuff is worse than second-hand smoke."

I closed my eyes and held my breath while she sprayed half the bottle on my head. By the time she was done, I was sure that if someone lit a match, my whole head would light on fire.

"Now, just one more…" She twisted a chunk of my hair and shoved one of those hair clips into it hard enough to make me wince. "There. Done."

I tried to move to see, but Marco pressed his hand into my shoulder. "Not so fast, hermosa. I'm not done yet. You don't want to get out there half done. I have my reputation at stake."

Pressing my lips together, I stayed still lest he

poke me in the eye with the brush. He applied some kind of liquid to my lips, and I was told to blot it before Marco announced he was done.

"What do you think?" Marco asked Michael who turned his eyes from the room and back to me.

The way he stared at me made me self-conscious. I hadn't even seen what they'd done, and he was already making me worry that it was bad. With a small lift of his chin, Michael stated, "It is acceptable."

"Well, that's high praise if I heard any." Marco grinned at Lisa before they moved my chair around to face the mirror.

"Wow," I gaped as I stared at my reflection.

Now, I wasn't a big person for hair and makeup. For me, the less trouble, the better. If it takes me more than five minutes to do, then it wasn't worth it. However, what Marco and Lisa did to me was nothing short of spectacular.

Lisa had curled my hair so that it rippled down from my head in waves then pinned one side of it up so that it looked like I was some sort of mermaid in mid-serenade. Marco had complimented her work on my hair with green and blues on my eyes and a shimmering sheen on my cheeks. My lashes were long and voluptuous, and my lips pouty and covered in a pale pink gloss.

I was a fucking fairy princess.

"You like?"

I turned my gaze away from the mirror to Lisa's impatient gaze. Nodding, I jumped out of the chair and hugged her. "Like it? I love it! Thank you so much." I gave Marco a hug as well before moving toward Michael.

"Hold on now, missy." Lisa grabbed my arm and pulled me back. "We're not done yet. The boss man said the whole shebang. That includes wardrobe too." She winked and pushed me toward another section filled with clothes and two arguing twins.

"Hey!" Lisa snapped her fingers to get the twins' attention. "This is Jane. Andre said to hook her up, so let's make her feel at home, 'kay?"

The twins, two women with sharp features and completely different hair and clothing styles, turned as one.

The first one with white blonde hair with a black underlayer held her hand out. "Nikki." I shook her hand and then glanced at the other twin who hadn't offered me a hand or a name. "This is my sister, Tracy."

Tracy's nose shifted even higher in the air, her auburn hair, a stark contrast to her sister's but I couldn't figure out who's was out of a box they were so well, blended with her features.

"So, you're who the boss is screwing this week?" Tracy snipped. She glanced me over and sniffed as if she found me lacking.

"Uh, no." I held my hands up and backed away from them. "I'm not…" My back bumped into a familiar chest, and I relaxed against Michael.

The twins' eyes moved up to the angel behind me and seemed to change their attitude. Tracy gave Michael a sultry smirk. "Why, hello there. Are we dressing this delicious being?"

"Oh, boy." Lisa snorted and rolled her eyes. "Stop drooling all over your Jimmy Choo's and dress this woman." She snapped her fingers, knocking the twins out of their stupor.

With a sigh of reluctance, Tracy and Nikki turned their eyes back to me. They circled me like vultures as their heavily made-up eyes took in every inch of me.

"Well, at least you aren't a piggy." Nikki poked at my side, making me flinch.

"You are a bit bustier than the others, so we'll have to see if we have anything that'll fit…" Tracy added, wasting no time reaching out to grab at my chest.

Frowning and already getting severely pissed off, I jerked out of her reach. "Hey, buy me a drink at least first, would ya?"

Blinking up at me, Tracy seemed confused by my outburst which made Marco chuckle. "Don't mind them. They are used to having their hands all over the pretty puntas. It's nothing personal."

My lips twisted into a frown, but I didn't argue further as they started pulling things from their clothing racks and tossing them at me. When Lisa and Marco turned to leave, I squeaked at them.

"No! Don't leave me here with…" I lowered my voice a tad bit as the twins argued over a piece of clothing. "… the neurotic twins."

"Oh, you'll be fine," Lisa said in an effort to calm me, waving a hand. Marco seemed a bit more anxious than her to leave, his eyes darting down the row and checking his watch.

"Does he need to pee?" I asked as I raised an eyebrow.

Michael interrupted Lisa's answer. "He is waiting for the female over there."

All our eyes shot to the strawberry blonde female dressed in a sheath dress and carrying a tray of coffee cups. She was a cute little thing, maybe even more out of her element than me. I watched with growing amusement as her foot caught on a table cloth, and her tray went flying in the air.

Marco dashed toward her but was too late. The coffee spilled everywhere, I admit I cried a bit inside at the sight, and she faceplanted on the ground. Marco knelt down beside her and helped her clean up the mess before offering her a hand to her feet. She shyly took his hand and stood beside him.

"That's Patrice," Nikki snipped, making me jump. Sneaky bitch. "She's a bumbling idiot, but for some reason, Marco is crazy about her."

"Are they dating?" I asked, glancing between the two of them with more interest.

Lisa snapped her gum. "He wishes. The boy doesn't have the cojones to ask her out. I don't know why. Not like she's out of his league."

"He'd be better off just getting a dog," Tracy growled. "At least, then he would only be cleaning up his shit rather than the hurricane Patrice caus-es." She and Nikki laughed, but the rest of us just looked at them like they were psychotic.

Well, Michael didn't. He had that blank look on his face like he'd rather be anywhere else than here.

Bet he was regretting not fucking me in the bathroom now. I snickered to myself.

"Alright, enough with the boring stuff," Tracy announced. "Let's get you out of those bargain basket pants and into something fabulous."

Lisa giggled at that and patted me on the shoulder, "Good luck." She skipped down the aisle toward Patrice and Marco and left me with the twins.

Wincing at the two of them, I had a thought. The set of *The Shining* had to be more welcoming than these two. Or Hell.

4

"Alright, disrobe," Nikki commanded as she pushed me toward a curtained-off area.

"Jeez!" I scowled as her knife-like nails pinched into my sides. "You don't have to be so rough. I'm going. I'm going."

Nikki rolled her eyes and shut the curtain without a word, leaving me in a cube-like section of more curtains. Seriously, someone only needed to pull one of the curtains back to see all my goodies. I shook my head at the visual and quickly started to take my clothes.

I'd never been one for trying on clothes. I preferred to be comfortable. Which was why I was happy to stay in the same size since high school. It made shopping a hell of a lot easier. Though, if only the fashion industry would make all their cloth sizes match.

Have you ever gone to a store and tried on your size in one pair of pants and then try on the exact same size but in a different brand and have them not fit? Yeah. Not fun. If they wanted people – especially women – to buy clothes and a lot of them they should make the trying on process easier. Maybe offer alcohol or a valium before heading into the changing room.

I could use one of either right about now.

When I had my shirt over my head, my arms still in the holes, I heard Tracy's voice. It had a kind of purring lilt to it that it didn't have before when she was talking to me. "So, you're her… brother?"

I was embarrassed to say that I strained to hear what Michael would say now that I was out of sight. Would he claim me as his girlfriend or whatever it was that we were? A part of me that I loathed admitting I had really wanted to hear him tell her off.

"Who?" Michael's stern voice could be heard through the many layers of curtains just as easily as if I were standing next to him.

"What's her name?" Nikki added with a click of her fingers.

Tracy added on, "That girl we're being forced to dress. There's no way a girl like that is with a guy like you. You have to be her coworker or something."

"Why would she be anything other than what she is?" I could hear the condescension in Michael's voice and could practically envision him with his arms crossed over his chest, his eyes looming down on the twins.

Tracy giggled. "So, you're not dating her?"

There was a long pause. I shifted closer to the curtains and arched my ear toward them in case I missed what Michael said which, of course, was when it happened. I, ever the graceful being, tripped over my own feet, my arms, still caught in my shirt above my head, couldn't help me regain my balance, and the next thing I knew, the curtain ripped, and I was falling. With a yelp, I braced for impact.

Faster than humanly possible, Michael grabbed me before I hit the floor, leaving me trapped in his arms with my arms up at an awkward angle.

Grinning sheepishly up at him, I muttered, "Uh, hi. Thanks."

"Wow, you're fast!" Nikki gaped at Michael as he righted me to my feet.

Still wobbly, I grimaced and held my arms toward Michael. "Could I get a bit of help?"

Michael eyed me, and then a small twitch of his lips was all the warning I had before he began to chuckle. Nikki and Tracy swooned. When Michael's chuckle turned into a full-on bellow, I scowled. It wasn't that funny.

The twins giggled along with him, laughing at my expense. Nostrils flaring, I lifted my nose in the air with a huff and stalked my way back to the dressing area, determined to help myself. Michael's hand shot out as I passed by and almost tripped me once more, but he caught me with one hand on my waist, and the other grabbed my trapped hands and jerked me toward him.

Our faces were close enough that our noses brushed which shut the twins up real quick as Michael leaned into me. "I think I like you like this, trapped and at my mercy."

I snorted, rolling my eyes. "Of course, you would…"

"Perhaps, we'll have to try this one back at home."

His sudden, provocative words made me swallow any sarcastic words I'd been planning to say, and my heart stuttered. "Uh, what now?"

Michael pulled on my arms just a bit tighter, making the joints ache a little while forcing my body to bend toward him unless I wanted to pull my shoulder out of its socket. My breasts, clad only in my bra, brushed against his chest and my nipples hardened. Michael's eyes darkened, his nostrils flaring at my building arousal.

"Uh… what did you have in mind?" I licked my lips, my voice coming out heavy and low.

The hand on my waist dipped down to my lower back, caressing the swell of my ass. Michael's mouth brushed against mine. His expression read of pleasure and pain, but I would love every moment of it. Before Michael could explain to me what he had planned in that twisted mind of his, Tracy, of course, let out a low growl of disgust.

"Sorry, but could you not eye fuck each other here? We have work to do," Tracy snapped, not waiting for us to break up before grabbing a pile of clothes and shoving it between us. "Put these on and get out."

Michael took the clothes since my arms were

still tied up. With a frown and an intense urge to flip Tracy off, I lowered my arms and fought for a second to untangle myself. Once I had escaped my own shirt, I switched with Michael and lifted up the first article of clothing with a skeptical frown.

"What's this crap? It's more of a death trap than an outfit." I glared at the smirking twins as I held up the forest green top with zippers all over it. There were more zippers than material. If I put it on, my bra was going to show through for sure.

The bottom wasn't much better. Zippers, zippers, and oh just for a good measure a tiny bit of lace. Everywhere. What, did these designers moonlight at BDMS bars or what?

I gave Michael a disbelieving look which he returned with an arched brow, his eyes laughing at me. With a disgusted sound, I grabbed the bundle of clothes and rolled my eyes. "Fine."

This time while I was behind the curtain, I didn't lean in to the hear the conversation. I was too busy trying to figure out how the hell I was supposed to put this outfit on to pay much mind.

Was this the top? Or the bottom?

If I thought I hated trying on clothes before I had entered the ninth ring of hell. Someone up there was having a laugh at my expense. And I bet it was Lucifer.

I fumbled with the top and let out a sigh of frustration. "Fuck. Is it this way?"

"Nikki, here's that thing you wanted," a nervous male voice stood out from behind the curtain.

"Oh, yeah. Just talk to me about it later, not here," Nikki told him back, her voice a bit on the nervous side. The fact that she didn't want to talk about it here was enough to interest me not that she didn't have a winning personality as it was. Her and her sister.

"But I don't know what I'm doing." The anxiety in his voice made me pause. "He hasn't called me back."

"I don't care. I said not here." Nikki's voice became irate, and the male made a sound like he wanted to argue further, but then the distinctive sound of stomping feet resounded on the floor.

My brow furrowed, I wondered briefly what that had been about and then glanced down at the monstrosity of a shirt I was wear. My bright hot pink bra was on display between the zipper holes clashing horribly with the green. Ick. I reached back and unsnapped my bra, then fought to pull it off through the shirt sleeves. It was even worse on than it was off. The shirt stopped right below my belly button, but it was practically just strips of fabric zipped together with metal. The teeth were open right now, showing everything but my nipples. I zipped up a few of the zippers until it was at least decent before trading my skirt for theirs.

There was a fucking zipper over my vag. What were they hoping for, easy access?

Then, as if I had summoned him by the sluttiness of my outfit, Lucifer appeared in the changing stall with me.

"Holy shitballs!" I placed a hand on my chest and gasped, glaring at the asshole Devil smirking like a fiend. "Don't do that."

Lucifer in his Devilish glory wore a pair of pair of navy-blue slacks and a white button-up shirt. Suspenders and a matching bow tie topped the outfit off, and I had to smile.

"Guess we're both playing dress up today, huh?" But my question wasn't answered by him but by one of the asshole twins.

"You done, yet? I have other shit to do," Tracy yelled at me from the other side of the curtain.

"Uh, yeah. I'm coming." I gave Lucifer a side look, warning him to be nice, but his eyes were locked on my body. I could feel him mentally undressing me with that scorching look, and I would be lying if it didn't make me hot.

Fucking suspenders. Who knew?

On the other side of the curtain, Michael waited with hands in his pockets and his eyes on a small bald man a few booths away. I touched his arm. Michael's gaze swung back to me and then over my shoulder to Lucifer.

I always wondered how they were able to see each other. I mean, I understood it when they were incorporeal but when they were physical did that mean they still kept all their powers? I should figure as much because of the abilities they used to help me catch bad guys. But physically? Were they immortal? Could they die? I hoped I never have to find out.

"We should go," Michael said and then stalked away without waiting for an answer.

I gave the twins a nervous little smile and waved. "Thanks." I hope you choke on your own spit and die a horrible death, you soul sucking vipers.

They either didn't hear me or didn't care because they were already back to fighting over the pile of clothes they had on a table. Shaking my head, I turned to follow Michael with Lucifer hot on my heels.

"I know what you're doing," I muttered under my breath. "Stop it." I brushed a hand behind me, trying to dislodge the eyes on my ass.

"I must have fallen asleep because there's no way that you would ever wear something like that unless I begged." Every word dripped with seduction, and I had no doubt in my mind that had we been alone, Lucifer would have delighted in opening each and every one of the zippers of my outfit to find the skin beneath.

Forcing myself not to respond to him, I stopped next to Michael. "Where are we going?"

"That man before. There was something suspicious about him." Michael stared at the bald man and then his eyes snapped to Lucifer. "Why aren't you looking for Uriel? This is my shift."

Lucifer held his hands up with a lilt of his lips. "I'm going. Just wanted to check and see how things were going." His heated gaze slid over to me, moving up and down my form. "Obviously, it's going well."

I flushed and bared my teeth at him. Then realized I was doing it to thin air as far as everyone else was concerned and stopped. "Get out of here already."

"Oh, love, you pain me so." Lucifer clasped his hands to his chest, making him look oh so pitiful and adorable all at once.

"Lucifer."

Michael's voice made the archangel drop his hands and point a finger at his brother, giving the more serious angel attitude, "You better make me proud."

"Lucy!" I gaped, grinning.

"Seriously, she's practically gift wrapped for you." Lucifer gestured at me with a gleam in his eyes. "If you don't take advantage of that, then I will disown you."

Michael didn't even bother to respond. Instead, he gestured toward the way the bald man was going. "We should follow him. I have a good feeling he has something to do with the theft."

"Okay." I nodded, ignoring Lucifer who kept grabbing at my zippers trying to make them open with force of will while incorporeal. "Let's go. Lucy, I'll catch you later." I winked. "If you're lucky, I'll get to keep the clothes."

"Alright, alright, I get when I'm not wanted." Lucifer backed away and then pointed a finger at

me as he left. "I'm going to hold you to that promise." He let out a laugh. "Fucking lucky bastard."

Following Michael down the aisle of booths, I
watched the little rat of a man go from booth to
booth, sometimes chatting to one of the people
there and sometimes taking notes before shoving
them into his pocket. His eyes darted around the
room like he was afraid someone was going to
see him.

"Definitely sketchy." I finally agreed as the guy
left out a side door and into the parking lot.

On this side of the building were several trailers
all lined up in a row. The sun beat down on us as
we walked across the pavement, not really trying to
hide as we followed him. Not that the guy even
noticed either. He wasn't looking at us, he was
looking at his phone, and then he put the phone to
his ear.

Michael and I stopped by a set of trucks
unloading equipment. Pretending to be paying
attention to them, we eavesdropped on the bald
guy's phone call.

"I have it. Yeah. Right now." He shook his
head, rubbing a hand over his face. "No, I can't
wait. It has to be now. Tonight. One o'clock.
Marcello's. Okay, okay. Bye." He let out a long-frus-

trated breath before shoving his phone in his pocket and climbing into a trailer.

"What was that about?" I exchanged a look with Michael.

"Sounds worth looking into."

"Agreed." I inclined my head, then I saw Patrice walking over with a clipboard and marking off things as they came off the truck. "Hey, Patrice."

The mousy woman looked up from her papers, and her brows furrowed as she took me in. "I'm sorry, do I know you?"

"Uh, yeah, no. I'm a friend of Andre's, checking out the fashion industry. He told me to look around and then find you if I had questions?" I bullshitted in the hopes that she would believe me.

"Oh, okay. No problem. What can I help you with?" So trusting. Poor thing.

"That short bald guy." I pointed to the trailer behind us. "Who is he?"

Her head cocked to the side, and then the guy in question came back out. "Oh!" Her eyes widened. "That's Noah, he assists some of the designers."

"Really? Okay. He didn't seem the type..." I trailed off, not knowing what else to say.

Patrice tucked a piece of hair behind her ear.

"You meet all kinds of people in this industry. You'll be surprised to see the variety of characters."

"Great. Thank you." I grinned at her and then turned to Michael to whisper, "Come on, let's go. We have a date to get ready for... at Marcello's."

5

Michael and I barely got back to my apartment before he started to become incorporeal. He tried to open the apartment door for me, but his hand went through the handle.

"Weird. Never had that happen before." I placed a hand on his shoulder where that part of him was still solid. "Do you need to go now? Or…?" I trailed off, biting the corner of my lip to hide my smile.

After all this time you'd think I could just say, "Can you stick around so you can fuck me?" Really, I was a strong independent woman who knew exactly what I wanted and usually went for it, but these guys, these angels always brought out a weird part of me. Sure, I acted like a badass bitch, demanding them to do this or that, but really, a part of me was still in awe that they would even stick around.

Can anyone say childhood trauma?

Michael, the glorious being that he was, no blaspheming there, didn't even blink an eye at my request. Reaching for my face with his one still solid hand, he leaned in.

"Hold up now." I held a hand up, not sure what he was planning on doing. "I'm all for adventurous sex, but I'd rather not get kicked out of my apartment when the landlord catches us doing it on the welcome mat."

Michael paused, his brows furrowed. "We cannot have sex unless I have more of your blood. Unless… you'd prefer me to disappear mid—"

"Nope!" I chirped, loud enough that I winced. No way did I want him to go incorporeal in the middle of sex. especially since he already didn't have one of his hands. With my luck, he would go poof right before I got off.

With a nod, Michael continued his movement. I stood there stiffly, not sure how he planned to get the blood since I'd left my clothes from before in the car with my pin in it.

His large hand encompassed the majority of my face, and I leaned into the warmth from it for just a moment, my eyes fluttering closed. Michael released a small sound, sort of between a groan and a growl as his lips brushed against mine. While I thought we were in a hurry, he took his time, sliding his mouth over mine, nipping at my bottom lip until I parted my mouth for him.

Our tongues twined together, and I angled my head back to give him more freedom to navigate my mouth. There was a good foot difference in height between us, and sometimes it was a struggle to find the most comfortable position for both of us. Most of the time we managed, even if we ended up a laughing mess. Well, more me than him. Michael had stoic and domineering down to an art, a hot sexy art but an art none the less.

I grabbed at his shirt and could feel the magic or whatever it was in my blood wearing off because it felt different. Lighter, softer, as if my hands would plunge into his chest at any moment.

"Hurry," I breathed, not wanting him to disappear.

In response, Michael pulled my tongue into his mouth, and a sharp pain from his canines made me wince. He soothed the cut with his mouth sucking and rubbing it with his own. The hand that had gone incorporeal wrapped around my throat, buzzing as it pushed up against my chin. It was a dangerous and thrilling position that had me throwing my leg up around his hips and grinding myself against him.

Abruptly, Michael released me and turned his back on me.

"What the- What the hell?" I panted at his back while he opened the apartment door. "I thought we were gonna… you know?"

Once the door was open, Michael spun around and lifted me off my feet. I let out a small squeak and latched my legs around him like a spider monkey. His hands cupped my ass, squeezing and fondling the globes as he carried me inside. He kicked the door shut behind him, and it finally dawned on me what he intended to do.

"Oh," I let out and then again, longer and breathier when his fingers dipped beneath the short skirt I wore. "We only have a few hours before we need to be at Marcello's and—"

"Quiet," he commanded.

"I'm just saying that I wanted to call Mandy and get her to c… ah… um… oh God almighty, where did you learn to do that?" I threw my head back and dug my fingers into Michael's neck as he did something quite miraculous with his fingers. A couple of seconds later, I was screaming, my insides clutching his fingers like I'd die if he moved them. At that moment, I felt like I just might.

My back hit my bed before I even came down from my high, and Michael was unzipping the front of my shirt to expose the majority of my breasts, nipples included, to the room. Gripping my breast in a tight grip, the teeth of the zipper bit into my flesh as he sucked on my nipple. The sensation pulled at my lower regions, something that had always confused me to no end. My nipple wasn't anywhere near my clit, so how did stimulating one have anything to do with the other?

"Stop thinking," Michael commanded, pulling me out of my thoughts.

While I'd been lost in my thoughts, Michael had shed himself of his shirt and pants, leaving him deliciously bare to my roaming eyes.

"Glory to God in the highest," I muttered, licking my lips at the sight.

"Please don't talk about *Him* while I'm defiling you."

I snorted and giggled. "It is a bit like talking about your dad during sex, huh?"

Michael shook his head, his sky-blue eyes sparkling with humor. "You have no idea. Now…" His chest muscles flexed which drew my eyes away from his quirked lips. "Let's see how else I can make you sing."

I only had about a millisecond of warning before that wonderfully sinful mouth dropped between my legs, and I was once again praising his dad for making an insightful creature. They really should give the angels more credit. They were messengers and warriors of God, but nowhere did anyone say they were this skilled in other areas.

"You're thinking again." Michael lifted up from my lap and narrowed his eyes on me. "I'm not doing this right if you have time to think."

"I'm not, and you're not. I mean, are." I slapped my hands over my face and dragged them down, probably ruining all of Marco's hard work. "My brain just won't shut up."

"Then let's see if we can fix that, shall we?"

My gaze dipped to where his hand wrapped around his length, dragging it up and down in a quick motion. Mesmerized by the movement, I followed him with my eyes. Now, I knew how a snake charmer felt but in reverse. I sat up and replaced his hand with my own. Climbing to my knees, my mouth dropped down, and I took him in.

"God," Michael gasped, and I grinned around his cock.

If I could bring an angel to say his father's name in vain, then I took that as a compliment.

Michael's fingers threaded through my hair and held me to him, not pushing but not directing me, just letting me do as I willed. I stared up at his beautiful face, watching his eyes scrunch closed in pleasure. As if feeling me watching him, those eyes opened, suddenly locking with mine as he thrust into my mouth with a grunt.

I felt his muscles tighten first before he came. Was it weird to compare human cum to an angel's? If it was, then I was just that weird. It would have been cool if it was like something... I don't know what I'd even imagine it to taste like... I guess more Heavenly?

Clean. That's the only word that came to mind. Which wasn't sexy at all.

I laughed as I pulled away from him.

"I might still be new to sex myself, but I'm pretty sure laughing at a guy's dick is not a good thing," a familiar, laid-back voice called from the kitchen.

Michael and I jerked our eyes over to where Gabriel leaned against the counter, his arms crossed and a shit-eating grin on his lips.

Shaking my head, I wiped a hand over my mouth. "I wasn't laughing at him."

"Her brain won't be quiet," Michael interjected, giving me a pointed look.

"If you say so." Gabriel continued to grin like a fool.

Shifting off the bed, I searched the ground for something else to wear. I was not going to Marcello's looking like a hooker which was exactly what the twins seem to have intended.

"What do you have to report?" Michael didn't even bother to get dressed, comfortable enough in his own skin to stand in the middle of the apartment butt ass naked. I couldn't blame him. What an ass it was.

Gabriel stopped staring a hole in my exposed breasts and turned to Michael. It was a curious thing the way he suddenly went from fun-loving pervert to a soldier in a blink of an eye. His back straightened, his grin slipped into a flat line, and all humor disappeared from his face. "We caught up to Uriel in the ether, but he gave us the slip again. Lucifer has his demons searching the nether for him as well."

"And the protestors?" Michael asked sternly.

Shifting uncomfortably, Gabriel glanced over to me where I'd been pretending not to eavesdrop as I pulled on a pair of slacks and a ruffled blood red shirt. "They're still calling for her demise."

"What?" I choked, my eyes widening. My eyes darted between the two of them. "Now they want me dead? When did this happen?"

Gabriel grinned at me as if he hadn't just said all of Heaven wanted to take me out. "About the time you were sucking down Michael's cock."

I threw a shoe at him. Sadly, he easily dodged it. Turning to Michael, I held my hands out in front of me and pleaded, "What are you going to do? You won't let them kill me, will you?"

Michael's brows furrowed. "Of course not. They aren't completely unreasonable, and it isn't all of Heaven, only a third of them. The rest either don't care or—"

"Want to fuck you," Gabriel happily provided.

"Woah. Woah." I waved my hands in front of my vagina. "Three is plenty as it is, I'm not opening Janetown for everyone in heaven. There's only so many dicks I can handle."

"Janetown?" Gabriel guffawed, and Michael

lifted a brow. "Can I get a day pass 'cause I seriously need a vacation?"

While Gabriel and I giggled over my new terminology, Michael pulled his clothing back on. Once he was done, the angel came over to me and kissed my forehead, a sweet gesture that strangely made me frown. He'd never done that before.

"I have to go. Bring Gabriel with you to Marcello's." Michael held my hands and peered into my eyes. There was something serious about his face that made my heart race. "Please be careful. Uriel is still out there, and there may be others who come for you. The best advice I can give you is to not make eye contact with others unless you know for sure they are human."

I glanced between Michael and Gabriel, the latter nodding solemnly. "They can't touch me if they aren't corporeal though, right?"

This time Gabriel answered. "That's partly true. We technically not allowed to involve ourselves with humans, but they will use our involvement with you as an excuse to bend those rules."

"And we can affect the world around us, make things harder for you." Michael gave me a warning look.

"Kind of like how you can make it thunder and the ground shake?"

Michael nodded. "Precisely."

"You should bring Mandy with you too," Gabriel suggested, "as an extra precaution."

I sighed and grabbed my phone from where I'd dropped my purse inside the door. "Well, it's a good thing I had already planned on calling her in the first place. She's going to ask questions, you know. Lots of them."

"That's fine." Michael cut his gaze to Gabriel. "Keep an eye on her."

Then he was gone, leaving me with Gabriel, a ringing phone, and a bad feeling in my stomach.

"What do you want now? I have a pile of paper-work on my desk, and O'Connor is in one of his moods again." Mandy's voice came over the line with a hint of exasperation in it.

Frowning at where Michael had once stood, I mumbled, "That's too bad."

There was a pause, and then Mandy asked, "What's wrong?"

I looked to Gabriel in a panic. "Uh, nothing. Why would you think something was wrong?"

"Uh, because you didn't make a wisecrack about O'Connor," she astutely noted. "So, either you're hurt, sick, or something bad happened. Which one?"

I let out a nervous chuckle. "Oh, you know. It's just that time of the month. Hey, while I have you on the line, what are you doing for lunch?"

Mandy sighed. "Contemplating my sad existence, why?"

Working as a detective at the Blessed Falls Police Department was hardly a sad existence, but I let her have that one. Her partner, O'Connor, was a dick and in serious need of a personality makeover. Mandy and I have been best friends since elementary school, and we knew each other like the back of our hands. It wasn't surprising Mandy knew something was wrong with me right off the bat. However, I wanted to keep her out of my supernatural political problem as much as possible.

"I have a case I'm working on and would like some backup," I said truthfully. "I have to find this golden trophy for a rich guy running that fashion competition this weekend. Think you can help me out?"

"You mean Andre Belmont?" Mandy let out a high-pitched squeal, and I could practically see her bouncing up in down in her seat. Mandy might be the serious one of the two of us, but even she apparently wasn't immune to hot rich guys.

"How do you even know him?" I asked, a bit bemused. Gabriel pointed at the clock, and I held a finger up.

"Well, that's a long story." She giggled like a flustered school girl. Weird. Andre was hot, but Mandy rarely got this worked up over a guy.

"You can tell me when you meet me at Marcello's."

"Ooo, fancy." I heard some rummaging around, the sounds of the precinct filling in from the background. "Just give me five minutes, I'll be heading that way."

"Okay, I'll be there. And Mandy," I waited until she let me know she was still there, "don't dress like a cop."

"I don't dress like a cop."

Rolling my eyes, I huffed a laugh. "Yeah, you do."

"Fine, I do, but if I'm dressing up, you better be putting out."

I chuckled, winking at Gabriel. "Oh, you know I'm good for it."

"I expect flowers too."

"Pfft. What? Do you think I'm made of

money?" Mandy laughed, and I hung up before she could give me a quip about my parents' money. No need to start an argument.

Gabriel moved away from his place at the counter and eyed me up and down. "So, I'd ask for some of the good stuff, but I don't think we have time for what I want to do to you."

I flushed, my body pulsating at his words. "Good idea."

6

Marcello's was one of the, well, I wouldn't say best, more like the only Italian restaurants in Blessed Falls. That meant they could charge up the ass for cold spaghetti and cheap wine. However, it was all worth it for the garlic bread.

"Mmmm," I groaned as I sank my teeth into the warm buttery goodness. It was like a parade on Ecstasy were having a party in my mouth and that party came with a ton of orgasms. Like, someone had taken ordinary bread and poured liquid love onto it and baked it to perfection. Really, they should write symphonies for this bread. Sonnets. Poems. Sappy love songs that would be played at weddings just to this bread.

"Oh, god. I can see your mind going crazy. Please just stop." Mandy who sat across from me at the table rolled her eyes and tried to hide her face in her hand. She'd come to meet me for lunch in the middle of work. So, she was dressed for the office. Slacks and a polo shirt, along with her badge and gun on her hip. For someone who was supposed to be good at staking people out, she sure didn't know how to dress the part.

"I can't." I hummed, taking another delectable bite. "It's just so damn good. It's better than sex."

"Even angel sex?" Mandy arched a brow curious instead of embarrassed for a moment.

Opening my eyes, I peered over at Gabriel who seemed more than interested in hearing what I had to say to that. Well, I couldn't very well kill his ego over a piece of bread.

I sighed, sitting the bread back down. "Okay, not quite there but close. Still you have to admit. It's oh-god-oh-god," I grabbed my hair and chest in a mock 'When Harry Met Sally' moment. "Good." I smirked and picked my bread back up.

Mandy made a disgusted sound. "Please, stop that. People are staring."

Smirking, I darted my eyes around the restaurant. Circular tables covered in red table cloths sat around the room. Some of them were stained, but nobody cared, or if they did, they didn't complain. Small LED tea lights sat in the middle of the table encased in painted glass cups. Being lunchtime, most of the tables were filled, and the air was filled with chatting guests taking time out of their busy days to have lunch.

No one even blinked an eye at Mandy, Gabriel, and me sitting in the middle of the room. Well, Mandy and me. Gabriel wasn't exactly visible.

"I don't agree." Gabriel grinned, leaning on his elbow as he grinned at me. "I find it extremely interesting that the face you make when you are orgasming is the same as when you eat bread."

Most people would be embarrassed to have your orgasm face told to your best friend but I was a stronger person than that. Plus, not like Mandy hadn't heard worse.

"Not just any bread," I told him through a mouthful of Nirvana, tipping it to him like a tea cup. "The perfect most wondrous bread in the world. No the universe. Even God couldn't make this good of bread."

"Ah, ah. That is blasphemous." Gabriel waved a

finger at me. "You don't want to piss you-know-who off. I like being here if you don't mind."

I pouted, fluttering my lashes at him.

Mandy's eyes moved to where I talked to what she thought was an empty space. "You know, it's a bit unnerving to see you do that. I thought you could make them... you know..." She waved her hand at Gabriel's chair. "Visible."

I lifted a shoulder. "He didn't want to be. I can't make him."

Gabriel snorted, and then his voice lowered an octave. "You could make me do a lot of things. However, I didn't think your culprit would wait around while I fucked you silly."

I flushed, a smile spreading across my lips. "Stop it."

Ignoring Gabriel's flirty wink, I glanced over at the balding guy who was sweating through his cheap polyester suit. Noah had arrived at Marcello's a few minutes after we had taken our seat. Now, we waited while stuffing our faces for him to meet whoever Noah was waiting for. I hoped it was the guy we were looking for.

The way he had been talking to Nikki, I had high hopes that it was an inside job and that maybe it had been more than one person. If this panned out, then I could get the trophy, get paid, and hopefully get laid.

"So, tell me about this case," Mandy said before taking a bite from her food. "You're looking for a trophy? I thought you mainly did stalkers and cheating spouses."

I scowled. "Hey, I do more than that." I stared at her and then grinned. "Sometimes, I rescue lost puppies and walk old ladies across the street between stalkers and cheating spouses."

Mandy and I giggled.

Gabriel watched with growing amusement. I wondered what he thought of this all. Did he have any best friends? Or just brothers in arms? Did he even have parents? There were so many questions I wanted to ask him but now wasn't the time to do it."

"Yep." I popped my lips at the end of the word and then took a sip from my cup. Yum. Drinking at noon in most cases wouldn't have been a good thing, but since it was all chargeable to Andre, I thought... what the Hell? It's wine o'clock somewhere.

"And this guy might have it?" Mandy angled

her eyes toward Noah but didn't turn to look at him like a true pro. Why couldn't I be that cool?

I shrugged. "Hopefully, but I'm not betting on it. He was acting sketchy at the Civic Center so..." I lifted a shoulder and dropped it once more.

I wasn't betting all my chickens on this farm but I had to start somewhere and if that meant I got a free meal out of the deal? Then I was all for it.

"Can't your little angels help you?" Mandy teased, swirling her fork in her spaghetti before shoving it into her mouth. The table jolted, and her water glass, no wine for her she was on duty, knocked over, spilling over the edge of the table. Mandy jumped up with a gasp before the water could hit her lap.

Gabriel chuckled and leaned back in his chair.

"Not cool." Mandy narrowed her eyes on the empty space.

Licking a drop of wine from the edge of my mouth, I giggled. "You shouldn't make fun of them. Not cool."

Mandy sat back down with a scowl as our waiter rushed over to clean up the mess. "Thanks." She offered the waiter a smile before turning back to me. The waiter almost swooned on the spot. Mandy had that kind of effect on people. Men in particular. She was a blonde boom shell with a gun. "Anyway, why can't they help you with this? Why me?"

"Would you rather be back at the precinct listening to O'Connor whine about his lack of sex appeal?"

"Can't I just want to have lunch with my bestie?" I cocked my head to the side. "Would you rather be back at the precinct listening to O'Connor whine about his lack of sex appeal?"

Detective O'Connor was Mandy's partner and a real pain in the ass. He had a tragic love life and was constantly taking it out on Mandy and those around him. If I was her, I'd have eaten my gun before the day was over. However, Mandy had always been the more patient one. She was my best friend after all.

Mandy rolled her eyes. "You are really looking to get yourself arrested one of these days."

"Hey." I pointed my fork at her. "I have never assaulted him... just verbally abused him." I winked at Gabriel.

Giving me a small smile, Gabriel turned his head, distracted. He seemed to be listening to something.

"What is it?" Mandy asked me, looking to the empty chair and then me.

"He's on the phone." Gabriel jerked his head toward Noah.

Shifting slightly in my chair, I watched our guy from the corner of my eye. Noah had the phone pressed to his face, his mouth pinched into a tight line. I couldn't tell what he was saying, but I was sure that he was arguing with someone on the phone. For a moment, my attention was pulled from Noah to the same two angels from the other day.

They were sitting at a booth. Not talking just sitting there. At least this time they weren't trying to stand out. I glanced a look at Gabriel but he didn't seem to notice them. Or if he did he wasn't saying anything.

Well, if he wasn't worried then I wouldn't be. Yet.

"Can you hear what he's saying?" I shot a look at Mandy, and she shook her head.

I tried to listen in but I didn't have super hearing. But Gabriel did. He watched the man, not hindered by being corporeal and then his gaze got that far away look on his face.

"The person he's meeting isn't coming," Gabriel noted.

I jerked my attention to the angel. "What do you mean he's not coming?"

"I mean that I had a vision and the guy's not coming." Gabriel stood to his feet all of a sudden. "In fact, he's about to bolt... in three, two..."

Mandy and I jumped to our feet as Noah caught us looking and took off toward the front door. I started to chase after him, but Mandy grabbed my arm. "What about the bill?"

"Bad guy first, bill later." I shook her free and ran for the door, not waiting for her to follow after. I had a bad guy to catch and I wasn't going to let cold spaghetti hold me back no matter how good the bread.

Mandy huffed and then raced after me. The waiter yelled at us to stop, but we ignored him. We shoved through the front door and paused to search for the bald guy.

"There he is," Mandy shouted, pointing to where Noah was running down the sidewalk. We ran after him side-by-side, pushing past people staring at us. I could hear the waiter yelling at us from where he had followed us outside, but we kept pushing forward.

Noah fumbled with his keys as he made his way

toward an old beat-up Toyota. His beady eyes darted to us and back.

"You keep going, I'll cut around his car," Mandy instructed before taking off. She really pumped her arms and legs, making short work of the few yards between us. Man, I needed to work out more if I was going to be hunting bad guys.

"Having fun, pet?" Lucifer appeared on the hood of a nearby car with a laughing grin.

I shook my head at him. "I don't have time for you right now." I caught up to Noah just as Mandy whipped out her badge to show to the stuttering man.

"I didn't do anything wrong," Noah got out as he held his hands up, his eyes jerking back and forth between us.

"Then give back the trophy, and we won't have an issue," I told him, crossing my arms over my chest and putting on my best alpha glare.

"Trophy?" Noah's eyes widened as he glanced between the two of us. "What trophy?"

"He didn't take it." Gabriel appeared next to Lucifer and watched with a bored expression. I put my back to them, coming in on the other side of Noah so he couldn't take off again.

"If you didn't do anything wrong, then why did

you run?" Mandy asked, putting her badge up and moving in closer. Even she didn't believe this guy was innocent.

Noah sighed, his chest heaving up and down. "Okay, okay." He pulled a handkerchief out of his pocket and rubbed it over his sweaty bald head. "I was going to sell the list of judges for the contest to this guy. They wanted to make sure they won."

Chancing a glance over my shoulder at Lucifer, I lifted a brow.

He shook his head. "He's telling the truth."

"Please don't arrest me," Noah begged as he clasped his hands in front of him. "If I have a criminal record, no one will hire me ever again. I didn't know it was illegal."

Mandy let out a heavy sigh. "It's not but you're going to get in big trouble with your boss if you signed an NDA and broke it. They could sue you."

Noah's eyes widened. "You're not going to tell Andre, are you? I really need this job."

Eyes locking onto mine, Mandy lifted a shoulder. "It's up to you, this is your gig."

"Nah." I sighed. "No need to ruin his life just because he wasn't our guy."

Noah sagged and then his face changed. "The trophy is missing?"

Mandy and I exchanged a look. I clamped a hand on his shoulder and rubbed his shoulder vigorously. "On second thought... maybe Andre should know that he has a traitor in his midst."

"No, no." Noah shook his head, his face scrunching up in fear. "I won't tell, I promise. Just don't tell Andre. Please."

"Can't you just kill him?" Lucifer offered.

"No, I can't," I answered Lucifer which earned me a weird look from Noah. Before I could interrogate Noah more, the waiter appeared next to the car, gasping for breath.

"You need to pay for your food unless you want us to call the cops." The waiter snapped, holding our receipt out. "Now."

Glancing over my shoulder at Mandy, I arched a brow. "You want to tell them? Or should I?"

Mandy pulled her badge out of her back pocket. "I'm on a case, we'll be back in there to pay in a moment." The waiter gave Mandy's badge a suspicious look before nodding tightly.

The waiter left, and I turned back to Noah. "Now, which contestant were you going to make a deal with?"

"I... I don't know. I just had a number." Noah pulled out his phone and showed us. "I can't even tell you if it was a male or female. They used a voice distorter."

Mandy jotted the number down giving me a meaningful look. "I'll look it up back at the station. You should probably go take care of that bill."

I let out an exasperated sigh before nodding to Mandy. "Alright, I guess. I'll pay the bill, and then I have to go check back at the contest. Maybe there's someone there I can harass." We moved away from Noah letting him get in his car and drive away.

"Make sure that's all you're checking out," Mandy eyed the space behind me. "You still don't know the consequences of fraternizing with these things."

Lucifer snorted and moved in close to me, causing a tingle to go up my arm. "Angels. Tell her we're angels, not things."

I waved a hand back at him. "She knows you're not things. Don't get your panties in a twist."

"Oh, love. You know I don't wear underwear. Though, I could be persuaded to wear yours." His words heated my skin, and I ducked my head to hide my reaction from Mandy.

"Alright, I'll call you when I get something," Mandy told me, her eyes on her phone and not on me. "Thanks for lunch."

I waved at her as I made my way back to the restaurant. The waiter was waiting by the front door, clearly not expecting us to keep our promise to pay. I offered him a grin and pulled out my credit card. "Put it on the company card."

7

Once the check was paid and we were back in my car, I peered at the two angels following me. "So, how long do I get to keep you two today? Or does Gabriel need to leave now that you're here?"

"I don't see why either of us need to take off just yet. Michael. ever the champion. has it all under control." Lucifer grinned from the back seat, his arms thrown over the back of the seat as he spread out until he filled the whole backseat. "Unless you'd rather Gabriel leave us alone?" He wagged his brows at me with a sinful grin.

I rolled my eyes at him as I backed the car out of its parking spot. "You heard Mandy, we can't get distracted."

Gabriel made a sound that made me almost hit a car coming behind me. Jerking the car to a stop, I waited until the car passed by before turning to Gabriel.

"What?"

"Nothing. Nothing." Gabriel held a hand up and smiled.

"Don't start that," I growled as I turned my eyes back to the road and off the way too distracting angels. "I have stuff to do. She's right. I can't stop what I'm doing just to bang you guys." My lips lifted at the edges. "I'd never put clothes on again."

"That's okay with me," Lucifer said with a rumble in his voice that made my insides warm.

As much as that sounded like a good idea, I didn't think I could just spend my days in bed bouncing from one angel to the other. I had to eat after all. Though, food and sex were quite the pair...

"I think she's thinking about it." Gabriel smirked, his hand sliding over my thigh making it tingle. "Are you thinking about being with us all day? Every day? Losing yourself in the oblivion of our touch?"

"Wow, Gabriel." Lucifer leaned forward so that his hands brushed my shoulder. I glanced into the rear-view mirror and saw the wicked grin on his lips. "I never thought you had it in you."

"You're not the only one who can turn a phrase," Gabriel shot back with a lopsided grin. "Besides, you're not the only one who wants her naked and willing. Are you sure you don't have time for...?"

I laughed. "No, no. I don't. If I give in now, then I won't get anything else done today."

"Very well." Lucifer sighed and sat back. "Then how about some blood? I'd like to at least be able to breathe in your glorious scent. Touch your face. Kiss you." His words traced along my ears and my heart beat faster.

"You always have such a way with words." My fingers tightened on the wheel. "I sometimes wonder if any of them are real or if you're just..." I trailed off, biting my bottom lip. I couldn't believe I said that out loud. I wasn't that clingy, insecure person who needed reassurance that her boyfriends actually wanted to be with her.

"Jane." Gabriel reached a hand out while we were at a stop light, and his fingers brushed against my cheek. I turned my face away from the zings. "You're not just convenient. If that's what you're getting at."

I let out a hard breath and readjusted my grip on the steering wheel. "I'm not. I just… I don't know what I'm thinking. Everything is just so out of control with the other angels and, you know, Uriel. You guys aren't telling me much, and half the time, I can't get one minute alone with you that isn't interrupted by work or one of your 'sorry, gotta go' excuses."

"We're not leaving because we want to, pet." Lucifer moved closer once more. "We're doing this to protect you. We don't want anything to happen to you."

"Yeah, what he said," Gabriel added with a small frown. "Uriel isn't someone to mess with. When he wants something, he gets it."

"Fucking douche bag," Lucifer muttered, shaking his head. "At the moment, he is content with making chaos in Heaven, but he could very well come after you himself at any moment. We have to be prepared."

I went silent as I turned my car into the parking lot of the Civic Center. My mind raced with the possibilities of Uriel turning violent. I never expected to become endangered from being with the three of them. That hadn't been something anyone, even mom, who was all pro-angel, had warned me about. Now, not only did I have to worry about how I was going to keep the angels I had, but how I would keep the undesirables away. Man, did I miss when my only problems were being the crazy one.

Putting the car in park, I turned in my seat to face them. "If you're going to keep me safe, then I think you should be corporeal to do it. I mean, you can touch each other, but you can't touch me. What if one of them try to do some Final Destination crap and knock over a ladder that hits a bowling ball that ends up whacking me on the head in some freak accident? I don't want to be on the nine o'clock news, at least, not for this."

Lucifer and Gabriel exchanged a look before Lucifer inclined his head. "Very well, but we have to keep an eye out. That means one of us needs to keep a lookout at all times. No double hanky panky." He waved a finger at me with a hint of a smile.

Rolling my eyes, I half-laughed. "I think I can deal with that. Now…" I pulled the pin out of my shirt and pricked my finger. "Who's first?"

"Me." Lucifer moved closer, and Gabriel gave him a look. "Hey, I haven't gotten any in three days. Don't give me that look, mate."

Gabriel shook his head and crossed his arms over his chest, but he didn't protest.

The instant Lucifer's mouth covered my finger, I had to remind myself we were here to do work. No quickies in the backseat of my car. Of course, Lucifer wasn't helping the situation, taking his time sucking on my finger and giving me fuck-me eyes.

"Alright, that's enough." Gabriel edged in as Lucifer released my finger. "My turn."

I tore my eyes away from the devil and over to Gabriel. I had to re-prick my finger to get more blood flowing so he could have his turn. Thankfully, Gabriel was quick about it. A couple of tugs on my finger and he was done.

"Alrighty, then." I wiped my finger on my pants and tried to shake off the temptation of having them both there and physical. As angels, they were distraction enough, but when corporeal, their presence was enough to pull the attention of the most devoted human, male or female. I supposed it had something to do with their unearthly qualities.

Getting out of the car, I didn't wait to see if they followed me toward the building. If I wasn't allowed to get physical with them, then I had to limit the amount of touching that went on.

"Name?" the guard at the door asked as he glanced from me to his clipboard.

I shifted on the spot and frowned. "Uh, Jane Mehr. I don't know if I'm on the list... I'm here with—"

"Go ahead." The guard nodded and moved aside. Once I started past him, he stepped back into place. "Not you two."

I spun back around to see the guard's hand up, stopping Gabriel and Lucifer. "They're with me. They're my assistants."

The guard shook his head. "If they're not on the list, then they can't come in. That's the rules. Too many spies for the media." He locked eyes on the two of them with a stern glower to show that he was not going to be dissuaded.

Sighing, I pulled out my phone. "Let me just call Andre real quick," I told them as I held my finger up.

Lucifer smirked. "No, need." Locking eyes with the guard, he placed a hand on his shoulder. "You might want to check that list again, mate. I'm sure you're mistaken. Lucifer and Gabriel." Lucifer tapped the clipboard with a growing grin.

The guard didn't even look down at his clipboard before answering. "Of course, you are. Go ahead."

As I putt my phone back into my back pocket, I angled my head to the side. "What did you do?"

Lucifer held his arms out with a wicked grin. "I'm the Devil, love. It comes with some perks."

"Perks you aren't supposed to use, cheater." Gabriel brushed past him with a pout.

"Don't rain on my parade because you didn't get any useful skills when old dad created us."

Watching the two of them as we made our way into the building made me smile. They were a pair weren't they, arguing about what was right and wrong. Of course, the image of a little angel and devil on my shoulders came to mind and caused me to giggle.

"What was that, love?" Lucifer paused, his hands tucked into the pockets of his pants.

"Nothing." I grinned and kept walking, letting them trail behind me.

The moment the three of us stepped into the main area of the Civic Center, the sound lowered. Several sets of eyes swung our way as people stopped what they were doing to stare. Frowning, I glanced back at the guys and realized what they were seeing.

Two men, so night and day to each other, with Lucifer in his suit and tie ensemble and Gabriel in a pair of fitted jeans and a tight t-shirt. Light to dark, they were quite the pair. And I got to play with both of them.

Or eventually, I would.

I sighed and pitied myself as I walked away from them and toward the back room. To my luck, Andre happened to be coming out of the office just as I came over.

"Andre." I waved to get his attention.

The gorgeous man glanced up from his phone and over to me. His eyes scanned over my hair and makeup and then landed on my clothes with a frown. "I thought you were getting a makeover."

I shrugged a sheepish shoulder. "I did, but it wasn't really me. Thank you though. It was fun." Well, if you called getting a root canal without anesthetic fun, but I didn't tell him that.

"We meet again." Andre looked over my shoulder at Gabriel and then arched a brow at me. "And is he another one of your boyfriends?"

I didn't allow myself to become embarrassed. I lifted my chin and stared him down. "Yep."

Gabriel sensed the tension between us and stepped forward, holding a hand out. "I don't think we were properly introduced." Andre clasped hands with him. "I'm Gabriel. This is my brother, Lucifer."

Andre's lips curled up in an amused grin. "Gabriel, Lucifer, and Michael. Like from the Bible?"

Gabriel nodded as he crossed his arms. "Yep. Our dad was a big fan."

Lucifer snorted and chuckled. I shot him a warning look before turning back to Andre. "We wanted to talk to you about the judges. Can I talk to them?"

"No."

I frowned at the short one-word answer from Andre. "Uh, what do you mean no? They might have some clue to who stole the trophy." I wrapped my arms around myself.

Shifting from one foot to the other, Andre gestured to me. "I'm sorry, but only one person knows who they are, I don't even know."

Lucifer stepped closer to me and leaned in to whisper, "He's telling the truth."

I gave him a warning look. "I got that."

Andre gave us a curious frown, and then his phone buzzed. Lifting it up, Andre typed away on it, already distracted by whatever it said. "Have you had a chance to talk to the contestants yet?"

Dropping my arms, I shot a look behind me toward the lines of booths. "No, not yet. I was planning on doing it now." I gave him an apologetic smile. "I planned to do it earlier, but we were running down a lead."

"Alright, well, let me know if you need anything else. I need to go take care of a meltdown." He shook his head with a dimpled smile. "Designers. They're nothing but drama."

He started to walk away, but then Michael appeared in front of me. "Tell him to let us in the office again. I want to see the safe."

"Uh... before you go…" I quickly said to Andre as I placed a hand on his arm. He looked down at it and then to me with a grin. I dropped my hand. "I need back in the office." When he arched a brow at me, I stuttered out, "I wanted to check the safe again. Make sure I didn't miss anything."

Andre smirked. "If you didn't want me to go, all you had to do was ask."

8

Ignoring the daggers of pure hatred coming from the angels, I followed Andre into the office. Well, all but Lucifer. He only seemed amused by the whole thing.

"So, here's the safe." Andre waved a hand at the table where the safe sat on the floor. He scratched at the side of his face and frowned. "I don't know what you expect to find but have at it. I'll be back after I deal with this disaster." He held his phone up with a wry grin.

Once he was gone, I turned to Michael. "Want me to make you solid?"

"No," Michael clipped. "I'm not staying. I just remembered something." He angled his head to the side, and his pale blue eyes searched the area.

"I don't like that guy," Gabriel muttered as he moved closer to me. His hand slipped around my waist, and he rested his chin on my shoulder. "He wants you."

"Of course, he does." Lucifer chuckled. "Who wouldn't?"

I flushed, shifting uncomfortably. "Guys, you're making me blush."

"What are you doing here, Michael?" Lucifer asked with a frown. "I thought you were keeping an eye on Uriel."

"Helping as is my job," Michael quipped, his eyes shifting from the safe briefly to Lucifer before going back to it. "It's been replaced."

"What?" I asked, my brows furrowed. "What's been replaced?"

"The safe. Recently. The whole thing has been replaced." Michael gestured to where the safe sat.

"How do you know that?" I moved away from Gabriel and closer to Michael. Michael knelt on the ground and pointed at the ground.

"There. See how there are scraps on the ground just beneath safe?" I focused on the spot he pointed at, my brow furrowing. "Someone moved it."

"But it's bolted down," I argued, not quite

believing what he was telling me. "Nobody could have moved that."

"Well, they did." Michael stood. "This isn't the original safe. I don't know how else to explain it, but it smells too…"

"Clean," Gabriel ended for him.

My eyes shifted to him, and my heart stopped. Behind Gabriel and Lucifer stood Uriel. Long black hair hung around his face, and his beautiful face was pinched with annoyance. He hadn't changed since I'd last seen him. While the guys had chosen to keep with the times with their jeans and t-shirts, Uriel didn't give a fuck. A long dark robe covered his form, not doing much to cover his muscled form.

"What are you doing here, Uriel?" Michael asked from behind me, not a hint of worry in his voice.

Lucifer and Gabriel spun around and took a few steps back from Uriel to place themselves in front of me. It was nice to be protected but a bit of overkill.

Uriel gave the two of them a bored look. "Do you think you can protect your disgusting pet human from me? You're nothing."

Lucifer growled, baring his teeth at the other angel. "Watch your mouth. Or I'll—"

Uriel's eyes zeroed in on Lucifer. "You'll do what, traitor? You are no longer the favorite son, so don't puff your chest at me like one of these apes." He waved a hand around with a sneer. "I am not afraid of you. I don't even rate you on the map. You are less than a blip, a mosquito meant to be squashed for your insolence."

"And who's going to squash me? You?" Lucifer threw his head back and laughed before locking his eyes on him. I'd never seen him so angry. So intensely... I wouldn't say evil, but he was the Devil for crying out loud. He didn't get his name for nothing.

Uriel stepped toward us, and the two angels in front of me tensed.

"Enough," Michael's voice boomed in the small room, making the lights flicker.

I shot him a worried look. "Be careful, would you? We're not exactly alone here."

"Oh, yes. You wouldn't want the other apes to come scurrying this way." Uriel mocked with all the enthusiasm of a nun. "They aren't worthy of notice."

"Obviously, someone finds them so, or they wouldn't have made a whole planet for us," I snapped back at Uriel, tired of him downing my species. "It's you who aren't worthy of notice, or your daddy would have made you visible to everyone."

Uriel's eyes narrowed. "Do not think to speak to me. You're no—"

"Nothing. A flea. I got it." I cut him off before I held my hands up and puffed out a sigh. "You're worse than one of those Jersey Shore guys. All you need now is a spray tan and hair gel to complete the douche bag attitude."

Uriel disappeared and reappeared on the other side of Lucifer and Gabriel, just inches away from my face. "You will watch your tongue, or I will rip it out for you."

"Uriel." Michael's hand clamped down on his incorporeal shoulder. "That's enough. We have things to attend to."

"Which you would know if you weren't spending all your time on Earth with her," Uriel spat out, his gaze zipping back to me. "You are ignoring your duties every second you spend indulging in your sinful ways. All of you are." Those hateful eyes moved from me to Gabriel and Lucifer. "The traitor I understand but you, Gabriel?" He gave a disdainful shake of his head. "I thought better of you."

Gabriel shrugged and grinned. "What can I say? I'm a sucker for a pretty woman." He shot me a wink, and I grinned back.

"Disgraceful." Uriel made a face. "I should do you all a favor and remove the temptation." Before he could make good on his words, Michael dug his fingers into Uriel's shoulder, making him pause.

"Stop this, Uriel. You don't have the authority to do anything. We are not your enemy, do not make us one. Leave Jane alone."

Michael and Uriel stared each other down for a few more moments before Uriel finally broke away from the stare down.

"Very well, but they need to leave as well." He jerked his chin toward Gabriel and Lucifer.

Gabriel met Michael's gaze who nodded. He grunted, "Fine." Walking over to me, Gabriel took my arms in his hands and pressed his forehead to mine. "I will be back, don't count me out."

"Of course not." I lifted my head so I could press my lips to his mouth. Gabriel kissed me back harder, and his hands moved up my arms to tangle in my hair, deepening the kiss more. Uriel made a disgusted sound, but we ignored him and went on kissing.

After a few moments, Gabriel released my

mouth and stepped away. "Let's go. You coming?" he asked Lucifer over his shoulder.

Lucifer smirked at Uriel and crossed his arms over his chest. "Nope."

"Lucifer..." Michael warned, but Lucifer cut him off.

"No, Michael. I'm a traitor, remember? And besides, I don't live in Heaven anymore. I don't have to listen to any of you. So, you can very well bugger off, mate." Lucifer flipped him the bird in a very human manner, causing Uriel to groan.

"Just like someone as sinful as you to take on their mannerisms." Uriel sniffed and turned his back on us. "If you want to keep her safe, then you will leave with me now and never come back. Let the fallen son do what he wants, he always did."

Gabriel gave me an apologetic look before disappearing. When he was gone, Uriel locked eyes with Michael. The blonde sighed and gave me a reassuring nod before he and Uriel disappeared together.

When only Lucifer and I remained, I turned to him. "Has Uriel always been such a dick?"

Lucifer chuckled as he rubbed his jaw. "Oh, you don't know the half of it."

9

"Well, that was riveting." I sighed and scratched my head. "Any other siblings going to make a surprise appearance with a stick up their ass?"

Lucifer chuckled and leaned against a nearby table. "God, I hope not."

"What about the safe?" I threw a hand toward the metal box. "What do you think happened?"

"Eh... how should I know? Unless it can talk, I couldn't really tell you." Lucifer offered me a sideways grin. "But Michael was wrong."

"What?"

"It's not bolted down." Lucifer nodded towards the safe. "It might have been at one point, but it's not now."

I knelt and bent down to look underneath the safe. After a moment's inspection in the gap between the feet, I found one of the holes where a bolt should have secured it to the ground, but there was nothing protruding from the safe. He was right. It wasn't bolted down. At least, not anymore.

A low groan sounded behind me, and I froze. Grinning to myself, I said over my shoulder, "Stop staring at my ass Lucifer."

"I cannot help that my eyes wander to the perfect view in the room," Lucifer purred from behind me. "And your glorious ass is quite the view."

I chose not to comment on that assessment and focused on work instead. "So, who do you think was strong enough to switch out the safe?"

"Maybe they used that lift over there."

I glanced up to see where Lucifer pointed at a dolly. "Well, let's see." I stood and walked over to it. Grabbing the handle, I brought it over to the safe. Shoving it under the bottom of it, I tried to lift it up. After a moment or two of straining, I gave up with a huff. "Nope. Not someone like me."

"You just need a man's touch is all." Lucifer smirked as he shifted up beside me.

"Oh? You're an angel, not a man."

"Same difference."

"Uriel would say different," I muttered, glancing away from him.

"Hey." Lucifer cupped my chin and turned it back to him. "Ignore him. He doesn't know what he's talking about. He would be banished here on Earth with me as well if his nose wasn't so far up our father's butt. He makes the word brown noser sound like a compliment."

"Hmmm." I let him hold on to my face for a moment before pulling away. "Well, brown noser or not, he has no love for humans or you for that matter. Why is that?"

Lucifer snorted and turned his head away. "Like the douche bag said, I'm not exactly the favorite son, and they have promoted the hatred of me up there."

I frowned. "But Michael and Gabriel..."

"... aren't sheep following the herd," he finished for me. "They know better and were there when I fell or, well... was banished. They know better. Just like you." He tapped me on the nose.

"Oh, do I?" I arched a brow.

Instead of answering me, he took the dolly from me and tried to lift the safe. When he pulled it up with barely a strain, he raised a brow. "See? Easy."

"But would it be easy for a normal human male to do?" I countered, pointing a finger at him. "Could they do it?"

Lucifer dropped the safe back down and then gave me a pensive look. "I'm not sure. Not any normal sized male. He'd have to be a bigger man, lots of muscle." He held his arms out to make himself seem bigger.

I thought about it for a second and then shook my head. "I don't know anyone like that. Maybe Andre does. Come on." I started for the door, but Lucifer grabbed my hand, pulling me back to him. I giggled. "What now?"

"You know, it's been a while since we've been alone together."

I huffed a laugh. "What does that matter?"

Lucifer wrapped his arm around my waist, his palm heavy on my hip. "It means that I have you all to myself and I plan to take advantage of that." He trailed his fingers up my shoulder and then brushed his thumb across my lower lip. "Savor every second I have left."

He said it like he thought those seconds were limited. Like we weren't going to get to be together always. That might be true, but I didn't want to think about it right now.

So what if our time was limited? I mean, I was human. They're angels. What kind of life could we really have together?

Stealing little moments here and there, being together when work and life allowed it. The sad thing was that I could imagine us growing old together, having children, going for picnics on lazy Sunday afternoons. It was what every person wanted, to be with the ones they love.

But that won't ever happen for us. They were angels. Eventually, the other shoe was going to drop, and they weren't going to be able to be with me. Or maybe I'll fall in love with a human. I should. That would be the smart thing to do.

"Jane, love." Lucifer's voice pulled me out of my thoughts. "What are you thinking about?"

Turning my head toward him, I let a soft smile slid up my lips. "Nothing. I'm fine." As I twisted around, I allowed my smile to widen as I slipped my arms around his waist. I angled my head back and stood up on my toes slightly to graze Lucifer's lips with my own. "As much as I'd love to get naked with you right now, I'd rather not have my client walk in on us and lose this commission."

"Who said anything about getting naked?" Lucifer's lips curled up at the edges against mine as he held me closer, his hand moving down my back to press me hard into his arousal. "I could make us both very happy, and we wouldn't have to take anything off at all." One of his legs slid between mine, and I groaned at the friction it caused. "I just need five minutes."

"We don't have five minutes."

Lucifer shifted me hard against him. I gasped as I pulled my mouth away from him. He took that moment to dip his head down to my neck, kissing and licking up my throat. I grabbed at him, arching myself against him as he thrust his hips faster. On a hard thrust, my eyes jolted open, and I stared up at the ceiling.

That was when I saw it. A break in the case.

"Wait, wait!" I stopped moving against him and pointed over his shoulder, my eyes widening with excitement. "Is that what I think it is?"

Lucifer growled and shifted to look where I was pointing. "It's a camera. So bloody what? I'm more worried about what's in your pants."

I shoved at his shoulder with an eye roll. "Jeez, horny much?"

"Always, love. Always."

My face lit up at his words, but I ignored them. I moved away from him and crossed the room.

"That camera would have caught who moved the safe on tape, right?"

Lifting a shoulder, Lucifer stroked a hand over his chin. "I suppose it would have. Have you asked your client? Andre."

I gave him a sideways look. "Why do you say his name like that?"

"Come on, he wants you. It's clear." Lucifer watched me as if expecting me to say something about it.

Instead, I shrugged. "I'm hot shit, everyone human or angel wants a piece of this ass." I winked and grinned at him before moving toward the door. "Come on, let's go check out those tapes before I make you finish what you started."

"No complaints here." Lucifer's laughter followed me out of the office and into the main arena.

10

"Love, you know I would follow you to the ends of the earth but where are we going?" Lucifer asked as he trailed slightly behind me. A glance over my shoulder showed him with his hands tucked into the pockets of his slacks, his eyes moving over the different booths with bemused interest.

While Lucifer was looking around, it wasn't hard to see the not-so-subtle gawking as the women and men working the contest pointed in his direction. I hadn't seen the neurotic twins yet, but I was sure they would have hit on Lucifer within a millisecond of spotting him.

A pang of jealousy hit my heart. I wiped it from

my face and turned my gaze forward before Lucifer could see it. "I'm looking for Andre. We need to check the security cameras."

I wasn't good at hiding my emotions, even more so with an ethereal being who could literally smell your lies. However, more and more I realized that as much as I wanted to claim these gorgeous angels as mine, I might not get to keep them, so my jealousy was a moot point. They weren't mine to keep, and I needed to distance myself from getting too emotionally attached. No matter what Gabriel said before.

"Well, if we don't find him soon, I'm going to have to take off." Lucifer's expression narrowed. "The pheromones wafting off theses humans is giving me a headache."

I snorted. "Can angels get headaches? Aren't you above that?"

"Believe me, we can, and we do." Lucifer lifted his fingertips to the sides of his forehead. "We may be higher beings, but even we have weaknesses. Mine happen to be horny humans and polyester."

I giggled and shook my head at the wonder that was the Devil. "You know, if I told anyone that I knew the literal Devil and even explained an inch of what I know about you, they would say I was full of shit."

"What do you mean?"

I didn't answer Lucifer as I caught sight of Andre's blonde curly head and held my hand up. Pushing up to my tiptoes, I cupped my hands over my mouth. "Andre!"

Andre's head jerked up from where he was looking over some material, one of his hands in his slack pockets as well. Hmmm. I wondered if it was a suit thing. Andre lifted a hand in my direction and gave me the one-minute finger and then turned back to the person he was talking to.

Spinning back around to the waiting devil, I smiled softly. "I don't have to tell you what the world paints you out to be."

"Pfft. Please don't tell me you're talking about that horns on the head and a long pointy tail bit?" He rolled his eyes and pressed his lips together in disgust. "It doesn't even show off my best features."

"And those would be?" I arched a brow.

Lucifer's eyes widened in surprise, his hand going to his heart in mock hurt. "You mean, you don't know? My charming personality for one and my wicked good looks for two."

"Don't forget your humbleness," I quipped.

"I'll leave being humble to the less fortunate." Lucifer beamed and then leaned in to whisper into my ear. "I'll settle for being sinful. It's more fun."

A shiver of desire ran through me. As I offered him a coy smile, I murmured back, "You do it very well, I have to admit."

"Oh, darling, you haven't seen anything yet." He winked at me and then glanced over my shoulder. "Andre, I don't believe we have officially met. I'm Lucifer." He grasped Andre's hand in his, giving it a firm shake as he leaned in. "Devil extraordinaire, ready and willing to help you find what you are looking for."

"Thank you, but I'm surprised Jane needs so much help with what she does." Andre's baby blues moved from Lucifer to me. "I would think that the psychic thing would be more of a solo act."

I lifted a shoulder. "Sometimes, but you need a good support system, and the guys do more than just help me commune with the spirits. They also do other things."

Andre didn't say anything as he waited for me to elaborate.

"Like taking care of her baser needs," Lucifer helpfully supplied, making me flush bright red. "It's hard to find someone who is good with their hands, as you well know.

Andre looked like he was trying to figure out if Lucifer was being serious or not, but based on how he found me this morning, I figured it would be an easy answer for him. Not wanting Andre to linger on my extracurricular for too long, I decided to get a jump on what I wanted.

"Can we take a look at the security cameras?" I asked as I leaned into Andre's view to make him focus on me. "We want to see if there was anything on the tapes to indicate the safe had been moved."

"Moved?" Andre cocked his head to the side. "But the safe is bolted down, there's no way to move it."

"Actually..." I drew out and then glanced at Lucifer. "We discovered that wasn't exactly the case. The safe is new. Did you get a new one?" I watch his expression for any changes. Not that I thought Andre would be the one to steal his own trophy, but things were starting to point in the wrong direction.

As he crossing his arms over his chest, Andre shook his head. "No, it's the same safe that was here when we started setting up a month ago. Are you sure it's not bolted down?" He searched my face, hope in his eyes.

"No way, mate." Lucifer slapped a hand on his shoulder. "That safe is as new as they come, and unless angels came in overnight and replaced it, your whole safe has been stolen."

I covered my mouth to hide a laugh that I turned into a cough when Andre gave me a peculiar look. "Um, what Lucifer means to say is: are you sure you didn't order anyone to change it? Or maybe the owners of the Civic Center did it by mistake?" I sounded optimistic, but it would be too easy for there to have been a mishap like that. I wasn't that lucky.

"No." Andre dragged a hand through his hair. "No one ordered a new one, and as far as I know, they never messaged me about it." He caught sight of Patrice and waved her over. "Patrice, I haven't gotten any calls or emails from the owners, have I? Within the last week?"

"Ummm…" She pushed her glasses up her nose and then ducked her head as she checked her tablet. She clicked on several things and then shook her head. "No, no message or calls. Why? Is there something I should have caught? I apologize in advance. I thought I was being on top of things. We have all the deliveries and caterers for the big day set up. Then the drama this morning with the zippers—"

"Breathe." Andre placed his hands on her shoulders. The gesture made Patrice lock eyes with him and stop talking. "Remember to breathe. We don't want you to pass out on us again, alright?"

Patrice took a few deep breaths, nodding dumbly before she frowned. "I'm not fired?"

"Of course not." Andre let out a small chuckle. "I just wanted to check on something. You haven't missed anything. I promise. You're doing a fabulous job. Now, why don't you go take a break and then I'll see you back at Marsha's table in ten?"

Patrice took a few more deep breaths. "Okay, yeah. I can do that. I better get her a coffee before—"

"No."

Andre's sharp tone made her suck in a breath. Lucifer and I exchanged an amused look at their back and forth, a hint of a smile on both of our faces.

"I mean," Andre softened his tone, "take a break. No fetching. Just breathing. Relaxing. Remember what I said?"

Patrice jerked her head up and down. "I can't take care of others if I don't take care of myself."

Andre finished the last line with her, giving her an encouraging nod in the process.

"Good. Now, I'll see you in ten."

With a curt incline of her head, Patrice hurried away, her flats tapping rapidly on the concrete floor. When she was gone, Andre turned back to us. He scratched the side of his face and smiled, causing those dimples to appear once more.

"Sorry about that. Sometimes I'm not only the boss but a therapist too. Or so it seems. Now," he clapped his hands together and pointed them at us, "you wanted the security footage. Well, I'd love to say there's something to see because that was the first thing I checked when I found it missing, but there's no video of anyone taking the trophy, only me putting it in there the first day."

"Well, can we see it anyway?" I asked with a gentle tone. I was taking the diplomatic approach for once. "There might be a clue you overlooked."

"Of course." Andre smiled down at me. "I hope you do find something. It would make my life a lot easier if we get this whole matter taken care of today." Pulling a key ring out of his pocket, he flipped through them before unhooking one. "Here, this goes to the security room up at the front of the building. It should say 'Security' on the door. If Ray asks, just say I sent you."

"Thanks. We'll try and be quick." I took the key from him and placed a hand on Lucifer's chest. "Let's go, so Andre can get back to work."

Lucifer and I left Andre to his work and headed toward the front of the center. As we assed by the other booths, we quickly noticed people were whispering and looking in our direction. It seemed that word had spread fast about my guys and me. That was bad. If someone found out I was there for something other than to audit the fashion business, Andre's hope to keep the trophy's theft out of the press was slim to none.

"I wish you had the ability to make people forget," I muttered, turning my head to Lucifer. "This is one of those instances where not being noticed is a good thing."

"I wouldn't know, love." Lucifer grinned. He placed a hand on my lower back as we stopped before the security door. "I've always been the center of attention, whether I was visible or not."

I pulled the key out and stuck it in the door, turning it as I said over my shoulder, "You revel in it. Don't pretend you don't."

"Oh, I'm not. I am a firm believer in the idea that no press is bad press."

The door pushed open to reveal a large man in his late fifties sitting at a control panel and eating a donut. When we approached, he barely glanced up from the screens. This was someone who would not be running down any bad guys any time soon.

"Uh, Ray?" I asked as I stopped next to the large uniformed man. The guy didn't so much as blink at us. "Andre said we could look at the security footage from this weekend?"

When Ray didn't move, I shot Lucifer a look and shrugged. An impatient frown pressed upon Lucifer's mouth as he was clearly getting tired of the whole ordeal. Sighing, I leaned on the counter next to Ray's donut plate, ready to give him a piece of my mind.

However, before I could utter a word, the screens in front of us changed. The time stamp on the videos was for last weekend. Either Ray was freaky fast or magic. Nevertheless, we got what we came for.

"Let's see what we have." I waved Lucifer closer, my eyes locked on the screen.

As we poured over the hours of footage from the weekend the trophy was supposedly stolen, I was becoming more and more reluctant to admit that Andre was right. There was nothing there. No one save Andre had come into the office to open the safe. He opened it, glanced inside where you could clearly see the golden trophy, and then moved in front of the safe as he closed it again before walking out of the office.

The rest of the weekend... nothing. Not so much as a janitor.

"Thanks, Ray," I told the man, not that he gave any indication that he heard me. I sighed and followed Lucifer out of the office. "There's nothing there. How is that possible? The trophy is clearly not there now even though it shows that Andre put it in there."

"But did he?" Lucifer arched a brow. "Perhaps our dear old client might not be telling the whole truth. Perhaps he isn't so well off as he claims, and he nicked the item to get himself out of a bind?"

I gaped at him for a moment then clipped my mouth shut. "No way," I said with a shake of my head. "That's not possible. He has a limo, and he already paid our retainer. Clearly, he's not hurting for money."

"He might just be trying to make it look like he covered all his bases," Lucifer pointed out. "The trophy is worth a considerable sum. Your retainer is pennies in the couch cushions in comparison, love."

As much as I wanted to tell Lucifer he was wrong, the evidence was piling up against Andre which was bad in so many ways.

11

As we marched through the center, I searched for Andre once more. However, after looking everywhere I couldn't find him. I did find Noah, though.

"Hey, you!" I pointed a finger at the short, balding man. When Noah saw me, his eyes widened, and his face began to splotch. His eyes darted from side to side like he was ready to bolt at any moment.

"What are you doing here?" he croaked out as he wrung his hands in front of him. "I thought you were going to leave me alone."

I narrowed my eyes at him and gave him a real menacing scowl. He shrank into himself, almost until his head was in his shirt like a turtle. Unable to hold it back any longer, I clapped a hand on his shoulder and laughed as I dropped the tough facade.

"I'm not here to out you. I just want to know where Andre went. Help a girl out?"

Noah visibly relaxed, letting out a fast breath. "You had me going there for a second."

"I know right?" I giggled and shrugged. "Sorry about that. I couldn't help myself." I smirked at Lucifer who returned my gleeful look before turning back to Noah. "So, Andre? Where is he?"

Noah pulled a handkerchief from his pocket and wiped his face and head. "I haven't seen him in a while. You could check the office."

"Good idea." I nodded firmly and then clapped him on the shoulder, again making him flinch. "Sorry, thanks."

As Lucifer and I headed to the office, the Devil leaned in and whispered, "You're almost as bad as I am. Are you sure there isn't a bit of wickedness in you?"

I gave him a sideways glance. "Not right now, I don't, but that could change if you play your cards right." I offered him a wink and enjoyed the surprise on his face. It wasn't every day you shock the Devil.

As I opened the office, I found Andre exactly where Noah had said. I stomped over to his desk and slapped a hand on top of it, making him glance up from the papers he was scribbling on. "Answer me this, did you or did you not hire me to cover up that you stole your own trophy?"

Andre's eyes widened marginally, and then his eyes narrowed into slits, his lips pressed into a thin line. "Who do you think you are talking to?"

"Aha! So, you don't deny it!" I pointed a finger at him, getting more and more irritated by the second. "I am appalled by your gall, sir. To think that you would hire me in an attempt to cover your crime makes you not only a criminal but an asshole. I am not someone that takes being made fun of lightly."

Lucifer scoffed. "But you can tease everyone else." I forced myself not to look at him while I was staring down Andre. Thankfully, the billionaire didn't seem to notice anything out of the ordinary.

"I do not know what brought you to these assumptions, but I can assure you I am not trying to play games." Andre's jaw tightened. "The very fact that you would insinuate that I might be guilty of such a crime makes me wonder about your credibility and whether or not I should have hired you in the first place." He stood abruptly from the desk and circled around to face me. "I was under the impression that you were a professional and while a bit unorthodox with your methods and choice of associates, I had high hopes you would live up to your reputation. I can see, I was wrong."

I didn't let him intimidate me as I crossed my arms over my chest. "Maybe you did. Maybe I'm not what you wanted me to be, because I can assure you, I am not a crock. I have real abilities that my 'associates' as you put it," I waved my hand back towards Lucifer with a nasty bite to my tone, "are more valuable to me than any employee you have here. So, when they say you might be the very criminal I'm being paid to find, then I take it with merit. They haven't proved me wrong yet."

With a firm nod of my chin, I waited for Andre to counter. The businessman seemed to be thinking, his brows scrunched together between his eyes. Lucifer, ever the helpful tension breaker, slow-clapped and chuckled. I shot him a glare then noticed Andre didn't pay him any mind.

"I do believe my time was up before we entered the office, love." Lucifer chuckled once more and moved toward Andre. He leaned in slightly and sniffed the air around him. "Sadly, I hate to say anything to the contrary especially after that moving speech, but I might be wrong. He doesn't seem to be lying."

"He doesn't?" I said out loud before I could catch myself. I fumbled for an explanation for my out-of-the-blue question. "Uh, I mean... I'm sorry if we have made some kind of mistake, but the evidence points to you for every instance."

Andre's expression changed from confusion to suspicion and perhaps a bit tired. Rubbing a hand over his jaw, he sighed. "I can't say I'm surprised."

"You aren't?"

"No. There are plenty of past and current contestants that would love nothing more than to stick it to me. Stealing the trophy would do just that." Andre let out a bitter laugh as he shook his head he sat on the edge of his desk. "You'd think after everything I've done for this industry that they might actually appreciate me."

"Humans are spiteful little creatures." Lucifer frowned, his eyes menacing. "You give them the world and they will do their very best to shit all over it."

I snort-laughed and then covered it with a

cough as I wiped my hand over my face. "That sucks. Who do you think could have done it?"

Lifting a shoulder and then dropping it, Andre had such a look of utter defeat in his posture that I had the urge to go to him, like, pat him on the back or something. Maybe I could find some cookies. Those always made me feel better. That and booze.

"Man, I feel like such a dick now." I scratched the back of my head and offered him a weak smile. "Here I am jumping to conclusions when I should have just asked you about it."

Andre shifted on the desk's edge and angled his body toward me. "What is it that you found? Where are they by the way?"

I stared at him for a moment. "Who?"

"Your assistants or boyfriends, whatever you're calling them." He waved a hand around the room. "Not that I am complaining, but you are pleasantly uncharacteristically chaperoned."

"Tell him we're off fighting off those would take advantage of your delicious... attributes." Lucifer smirked as he slid his heated gaze up and down my form.

I flushed and tucked a hair behind my ear before clearing my throat. "Uh, they're around. They have other jobs too. They can't be with me all the time." I looked pointedly at Lucifer with a smirk of my own. "Or they get tiresome."

"I could see that."

Lucifer scoffed at Andre's comment. "He only says that because he wants what's in your butt-hugging pants. We're competition. Not that there is any." Lucifer adjusted his jacket and gave Andre an indignant look. "Can't compete with an angel, mate."

I wanted to remind him that Andre couldn't hear him, but I didn't know how to do it without looking like a crazy person. Instead, I turned my attention away from the big-headed angel and back to the flesh and blood man before me.

"Well, they keep me on my toes that's for sure. In any case, I'm going to head home for the day, but tomorrow, we can focus on the contestants. I have a good feeling we're going to find the culprit there."

I moved toward the door without waiting for Andre to tell me I could go. I was my own person. He might pay me, but that didn't mean I was at his back and call and right now I was tired and hungry. I needed a nap, food, and an orgasm. Not in that particular order.

"Hold on a moment, Jane. If you would."

I paused at the door, turning back to Andre.

Lucifer stood off to the side, not at all happy that I waited. "Yes?"

Andre shifted onto his feet and walked toward me. I'd be lying if I didn't say the sight of him, the gorgeous man that he was, didn't cause some kind of visceral reaction in me. However...

"I don't usually do this... mix business with pleasure, especially after being insulted." He offered me a dimpled smile. "But would you like to have dinner with me?"

"Dinner? With you?" I arched a brow. "You realize I have three boyfriends."

Andre only grinned broader as he moved in just a step closer. "I like a challenge."

Lucifer snorted. "Like he even stands a chance."

I found myself smiling despite myself... or maybe to spite Lucifer for his blatant remark. I'd been telling myself this wouldn't last after all. At some point, Uriel will get his way, and I'll be dead, or they will leave me. Either way, I ended up alone. I shouldn't turn down a prospective backup plan though I felt like a dick for the second time in a span of the last half hour for considering Andre my back up. I didn't know him more than what he has told me so far. He could be a great guy, a 'wonderful best thing I will ever have' kind of guy. And if it doesn't work out well at least, I could say I vetted him for Mandy before she took a whack at him.

"Sure," I heard myself saying, and seeing Lucifer clamp his mouth shut out of the corner of my eye only made me bolder. "I'd love to have dinner with you."

ndre and I walked out of the Civic Center together with the eyes of many of the workers on us. None of them were as intense as the feel of the Devil's gaze boring into my back.

I'd had expected him to put up a fight. To throw a fit. Maybe even just leave, but in his usual fashion, Lucifer surprised me. Silently trailing after us, Lucifer didn't make a single sideways glance or snide comment. I'd have been worried had he been corporeal, but as he was, he couldn't be much more than a nuisance.

"Where would you like to go?" Andre asked as he offered me his arm once we were out of the building. The limo we had rode in before appeared before us as if by magic. What would it be like to have someone know your needs before you? I'd have a lot less late-night taco runs, that was for sure.

Putting a hand to my rumbling stomach, I shrugged. "Well, my stomach is only worried about getting fed, so I guess it's gentleman's choice." I grinned up at him while he helped me into the limo.

"If that's the way you want to play it then, I will do my best to impress." Andre chuckled, and then murmured something to the driver before sliding in next to me. Lucifer appeared on the other side, placing me firmly between the two of them. Andre's warm thigh pressed against mine while Lucifer's caused the usual zinging tingles.

I contemplated moving or maybe even asking Lucifer to move, but then Andre was talking again.

"So, Jane." He said my name like it was a fine wine, not something my mother randomly picked out of the baby book. "Tell me about yourself."

"Was that a request or a demand?" I quipped, only partially serious. I might be letting him take care of me for dinner, but I ain't no pushover. The only commands I took were in the bedroom, and those were only when they came from angelic beings. Thinking about the latest session with Michael made my core pulsate with desire.

Lucifer tensed next to me. I shot him a look and shook my head. I hoped I got across the fact that the arousal he sensed wasn't for Andre but for them.

"A request, of course." Andre threw his arm over the back of the couch so that it pressed against my shoulders. "I'll start. I'm an only child born of privilege. A literal silver spoon in my mouth, if you will." He offered me a sardonic smile. "My family was, are, about looks and what other people think. They raised me to care for others, do charity, etc., even if it was only for the press. As you could guess, they weren't pleased when I branched out into fashion instead of becoming a business mongrel like my father and grandfather before me."

"You still deal with business," I pointed out, happy for the focus off me for a moment.

What the hell was I going to tell him? I hadn't had to tell someone about myself for a long time. Mandy and my parents already knew all my quirkiness, seeing things and all. And the guys, well, they were something else altogether. I was more worried about keeping out of the looney bin than impressing them. Then they became corporeal, and I couldn't think of anything other than getting laid... a lot. It wasn't until recently that I started to think of the future. Like seriously, actually think about it.

"True." Andre nodded and turned so he could place his hand on my knee. It wasn't an unpleasant feeling, but I wasn't sure we were to the touching place yet.

I shifted one leg over the other so I had an excuse to get his hand off me.

"Have you always lived in Blessed Falls?" Andre asked.

"Me?" I pointed to myself, taken off guard.

Andre laughed, a rumbling full-throated laugh. "I don't see anyone else here."

If only he knew.

The silence followed after that with no comment from Lucifer worried me. What? No, smart ass remark? I wanted to ask him but couldn't with the current company.

To Andre, I flipped my hair and offered a smile to hide my discomfort. "Except a small stint in college, yes."

"College?" Andre's eyebrows shot up to his brows. "You went to college?"

I scoffed, mock offended. "You think that because I'm psychic, I can't have a formal education?"

"Now, I didn't say that." Andre quickly backed up his words, holding his hands up in front of him. "Don't curse me. I promise. I just didn't think you were the type."

"One, I'm not a witch, I'm a psychic. I wouldn't know my broom handle from my cauldron. Two, what do you mean, I'm don't look the type?" I gaped as the limo came to a stop. "I could have a Ph.D. and you wouldn't even know it."

"Do you?"

"Well, no," I shifted in my seat and then added, "but I could. What makes you think I wouldn't want to go to college? My father is a doctor, I'll have you know. He wanted me to be one too."

"Then why didn't you?"

"Because having my work rule my life, wasn't for me." I winked at him before darting out of the limo once the driver opened the door to leave a laughing Andre behind me.

Once out on the sidewalk, I stared up at the restaurant before us. Large window panels lined the walls, tinted over so we couldn't see in, but the patrons could see out. Andre appeared next to me and offered me his arm once more. With a glancing toward Lucifer who wasn't watching us but looking around instead, I took Andre's arm and let him lead me into the low murmur of the restaurant.

Inside was just as interesting as the outside. Long, hanging lights hung from the ceiling. Their hue was low enough that it gave the place a romantic feeling, and the sultry playing music only added to the effect. My mouth fell open, and I turned to Andre.

Andre didn't give me a chance to get on to him before he jumped in. "Impressed?"

"Yes." I nodded primly but then pointed an accusing finger at him. "However, I think we have a misunderstanding about what this dinner is all about. This... is not a date." I waved a hand between the two of us.

"It's not?"

"No," I said with a clipped tone but then smiled to lessen the blow. "It is a business dinner. Which you will be picking up the check for."

"Well, that was given regardless of the situation. However... I think you should reconsider." I opened my mouth to argue with him, but he lifted his hand and touched my lips. "Give me until dessert to decide. Then you can tell me I'm wasting my breath."

This time Lucifer stopped pretending to be interested in the room around us and actually locked eyes with me. There was a weird emotion playing in those eyes there. I couldn't place my finger on what it was though I was sure I didn't like it.

I started to tell Andre no, but Lucifer finally spoke up. "Just go for it, love. See what he has to say. You never know."

My eyes shot back to the fallen angel, concern etched in my face, but before I could answer either of them, the hostess came over. "Just two?"

"Yes. Unless," Andre glanced at me, "you're expecting any drop-ins?"

I shook my head. "No, not right now."

"Two then." Andre held two fingers up.

The hostess grabbed two menus and then checked something off on her podium before asking us to follow her. We moved through the tables and booths until we came to a cozy booth near the back. Here, we were barely visible to the rest of the room, like we were in our own little world, closed off to the rest of the restaurant.

I hated it.

Andre thankfully didn't insist on sitting right next to me and took the opposite side of the table from me. I took my menu and used it as a barrier between us. "What's good here?"

"What was that?" Andre asked as he pulled my menu down to meet my eyes. "I couldn't hear you over this massive thing."

I smiled slightly. "I said, what's good here?"

"Oh." Andre glanced down at his menu. "Well, everything really. They have a bit of anything you would want. What are you in the mood for?"

I hummed and glanced down at the menu. Lucifer stood off the side, not taking a seat with us. "Well, I need some meat." The look Andre gave me made me flush and quickly amend my statement. "I mean, I need some protein. Maybe a steak?"

Andre nodded. "That sounds good." The waiter approached the edge of our table. "We'll have two steaks, please. Medium rare?" He glanced to me, and I nodded. Not quite dead but not mooing anymore. "And your best Chardonnay."

"Right away." The waiter took our menus and hustled away.

Andre turned his blue eyes onto me, and I felt the pressure ratchet up.

Standing up suddenly, I announced, "I need to pee." Without waiting for him to answer, I marched away toward the restroom sign. I need a moment to catch my breath. To get my mind in the right place. To talk to Lucifer.

When safe behind closed doors, I turned to the Devil trailing behind me. "What's your problem?"

Lucifer didn't meet my eyes, his gaze on the sink counter. His finger traced a path on the marble counter, his lower lip slightly puffed out. "There's nothing wrong. Why would there be?"

"You're pouting. Why are you pouting?" I poked at him, frustrated that my finger only went through his chest rather than getting my point across.

His dark eyes shifted from the counter to me, the vulnerability there made me take a step back. A Devil with a heart was a curious thing to see. "I don't know what you're talking about, love. I do not pout."

As he claimed it, he pouted even more. I'd have laughed had it not been so darn pathetic. I thought I was the emotional one in this relationship, I never expected my angels to even be a problem. God, did that mean they had man periods? Was I doomed to have all three of them syncing up and then bitching and moaning together about how they needed ice cream and sex?

"I'd say, you need to check your own bullshit meter because you, my dear Devil, are lying." I waved a finger up and down his form. "Is it because of Andre?"

"No."

Ah. There it was. That lip. So, it was Andre.

"Lucifer, Lucy," I murmured as I moved in close to him. The line of my body pressed against his, causing a delightful buzzing down my skin. "We're in a relationship, aren't we?"

He nodded.

"Then you need to talk to me." When he turned his head away, I shifted to stay in his view. "If you don't want me here, just say so. I'll leave."

"Do you like him?" There was no jealousy in his tone, but there was a vulnerability in the question that made me want to hug him.

"I don't know. I barely know him."

"But you want to have sex with him." That was more of a statement than a question, so I didn't offer up an answer. Andre was attractive, I wasn't going to lie. Had I played with the idea of doing the naked dance with him? Sure, but about as much as I did when thinking about petting a snake.

"I'm not jealous," Lucifer began, his lips twisting into an astounded frown as if he were surprised by that. "I'm not sure what I am. I have no problem sharing you with others. That's quite obvious." He offered me a small smile. "However, I'm not sure about sharing you with a human. What if he doesn't want to share you? What if you love him more?"

I let out a nervous laugh. "Who said I loved you?"

"Don't you?" Lucifer cocked his head to the side.

I swallowed hard. This was not a discussion to be having in a public restroom while I was on a kind of date with another man, let alone when the others weren't there to talk about it too. Still, I examined my options.

Lying was out of the question. He would know. Honestly, I hadn't thought too much on it. But now that I was on the spot... I did love them. Why else would I feel like we are on a countdown to doomsday? If I was still just having fun, then I shouldn't care that it might soon be over.

"Yes," I murmured, my eyes cast down as I was unable to bring myself to look him in the eyes. I'd never told anyone I had loved them before. Not outside of the usual high school sweetheart kind of way at any rate, and those were rarely true love. I didn't know if it was with them either. Could you be truly in love with three people? Three angels for that matter.

"Then go have your date or whatever that blasted man wants to call it. I'll meet you at home." Lucifer slid his fingers underneath my chin, and the buzzing urged me to look up. He brushed his incorporeal lips against mine, and I sighed into the barely-there kiss. Would we always be saying goodbye? And would the next one be the last one?

13

W hen I got back to the table, our food had already arrived. Andre sat there looking ever the debonair billionaire with his glass of red wine in his hand but having not yet started to eat.

Such a gentleman. I couldn't help but wonder if Lucifer would be the same way if he were here all the time? Right now, we only had stolen moments here and there, but to have the guys here all the time? Even I couldn't imagine how that would turn out.

Shaking my head as I approached the table, I offered Andre an apologetic smile. "Sorry I took so long. Thank you for waiting."

Andre set his glass down and waved me off.

"Not a problem. I'm used to being starved with my busy schedule." He laughed nervously, and I laughed along with him.

"What else do you outside of the contest?" I asked as I picked up my own wine glass for a sip. Yum. Holding back the urge to down the glass, I sat it back down and poured over my food. The steak was medium rare just as we ordered, which was rare. Most of the time it either came mooing or charred to a crisp.

"Well, as you know, I deal with buying the stock for several different big clothing chains." Andre paused to take a bite of his steak, he chewed it around for a moment before picking up his glass and washed it down with wine. "I also do some charity with hospitals and women's shelters."

"Wow." I gaped at him, quite impressed. "You just have everything figured out, don't you?"

Andre chuckled. "Well, I don't know about that, but I do have my business life pretty much taken care of... well, except for the trophy. Which I hope will be resolved soon." He gave me a pointed look that made me flush.

"Of course."

"So tomorrow? You'll come by the Civic Center and interview the contestants?"

"That's the plan." I shoved a juicy piece of steak into my mouth. As I bit into it, some of the juice dribbled out of the corner of my mouth. I grabbed my napkin and quickly wiped at my face before any of it could fall on my clothes. I swore I was an adult most of the time.

"I want to warn you beforehand," Andre continued, not noticing or at least not commenting on my little slip-up, "they are an eccentric bunch. Don't go in thinking they will tell you anything, let alone half of it be truthful."

I cocked my head to the side and smirked. "Don't worry, I'm a bit of a human lie detector. I'll get to the truth of the matter."

"Oh, really?" Andre's eyes widened and then a slow salacious smile crept up his face. "What am I thinking now?"

"I said, a human lie detector, not a mind read-er." I pointed out with an eye roll. "But if I could read minds, I'd say you're barking up the wrong tree, mister. Three boyfriends, remember?" I held up three fingers to remind him.

Andre lifted a shoulder and dropped it, like it didn't matter much to him. "Well, can't blame a guy for trying." The waiter came by and took our plates. "Anyways, two of the contestants dropped out today, so you won't get to meet them all. You might have to make some house calls."

"Would you like a dessert menu?" the waiter asked before I could respond to Andre.

Andre glanced my way.

"Yes, but for to-go. I'm wiped out." I broke the stare Andre was giving me, not wanting to give him any ideas. "I'll have the cheesecake."

"Nothing for me, thank you." Andre nodded to the waiter and then back to me. "Will that be alright?"

"What?" I asked as I struggled to remember what he had said for a moment. "Oh, yeah. House calls. Not a problem. I've been in tougher situations than that. Just text me their information, and I'll get it done."

"Perfect." Andre stood as the waiter brought my to-go bag and no check.

"Are we going to dine and dash?" I glanced to the retreating waiter and then to the front where it was packed full of people. "Because I'll admit I've done it before, but there's no way we're getting out of here alive."

Andre let out an amused snort. "No, we're not. The check is taken care of, don't worry. After all, I own this place."

"Ah, okay. Boss's privilege." I clutched my to-go bag a bit tighter. I had the urge to impress him as well. "Well, I work with the police on occasion, and I'd hate to have to get bailed out of jail twice in one month."

"Twice?" Andre's eyes lit up with amusement. "Do I even want to know?"

"Not really." I shook my head. There was no reason he needed to know that I assaulted the Pizza Grill's mascot for slapping my ass.

"Alright then, save it for the second date."

"Second date? But we haven't had a first," I countered with a smug grin.

"Ah, haha." Andre inclined his head. "Well, then, I'll have to try even harder to impress you." He took my hand and kissed it, like some prince out of a fairy tale. It felt strange. Unnatural. But I couldn't bring myself to make fun of him for it before we were pushing through the crowd and were out of the restaurant. "Would you like me to take you home or call you a cab?"

I waved him off. "Don't worry about me. I got it. Thank you for dinner."

"Very well. Until tomorrow, Jane." Andre climbed into his limo and was gone, leaving me on the sidewalk.

Well, good job, Jane. In your desperation to get some space, you were now stranded. Better call a car. Ugh. That was going to eat into my funds. I didn't even know where we were.

Pulling my phone out, I called the car service to pick me up. I didn't have to wait for very long before a lady name Terry picked me up in her cherry red convertible.

"You call for a ride?" She lowered her sunglasses to see me even though there was no need for them at dusk.

"Uh, yeah. Thanks." I climbed into the car with Terry and listened to her ramble on about how she became a driver. Something to do with an ex-boyfriend leaving her for her sister and stealing all her money. Since she was a student at the college, she didn't have much time to work so this was the only job that was flexible. By the time we got to my apartment, I knew way more about Terry than I knew about most people.

I thanked her, tipped her generously, and escaped up to my apartment.

Once inside, I brought my to-go bag over to the counter and pulled out a fork. With a more than eager squeal, I opened the cake box and brought a bite of the rich, dense, creamy cheesecake to my mouth. Before I could wrap my mouth around it though, a voice called out.

"You're not going to offer me any, love? Well, that's just bad taste."

I lowered the fork and glowered at Lucifer. He sat on the edge of my couch, his eyes locked on me and my cake. "No, get your own."

"I would but…" Lucifer held his hands open, showing that they were empty. "There's not a lot of call for cheesecake in Heaven or Hell. I'm afraid you'll just have to share."

I pouted as I glanced down at the cake. "I don't wanna."

Lucifer appeared at my side, brushing his incorporeal fingertips against my cheek as he whispered, "I'll make it worth your while…"

Fuck me. Well, I think that was what he was offering any case, but man, he had a silver tongue. It was almost good enough to share my treasure with him. Almost.

"I don't think so." I picked my fork back up and lifted it to my mouth once more. However, the puppy dog eyes Lucifer gave me made me pause. I sighed, dropped the fork, and pulled my pin from my shirt. "Fine. But you can't have all of it. Just a bite."

"Of course. Just a bite."

With that assurance, I poked my finger and let a good drop of blood form on the tip. Lucifer took my finger into his mouth, sucking it until my knees weakened and his arm wrapped around my waist.

Gasping, I shook my head to clear. "That's what they all say and then the next thing you know they've taken your virginity in the back seat of a Corolla." I picked the fork back up and offered the bite on it to him.

Lucifer's brows furrowed at my comparison but then took the fork into his mouth. "Hmmm. You're right, that is good." He licked the edges of his lips. On him, the gesture was much more obscene, and suddenly, the cheesecake wasn't my main focus.

"Is it?" I half-murmured, my eyes on his mouth, fascinated by the movements, each swipe of his tongue on his lips.

The fallen angel seemed to notice my stare because his lips curled into a wicked grin. "Here, taste."

He then cupped my chin and pressed our mouths together, slipping his tongue inside and wrapping it around mine. My hands found the front of his shirt, and I tugged him closer, unable to get enough of him from just one taste. I should be used to it now. Since day one, I'd been consumed by Lucifer and the others, unable to separate from them and keep my distance. Not that I had tried very hard, but even now, I wanted nothing more than to lose myself in his embrace, especially if this could be the last time.

Sensing my desperation, Lucifer pressed me closer. Our fronts melded together, and a delicious friction rubbed against my breasts. It wasn't enough. It would never be enough.

I tugged at his jacket and shoved it off his shoulders before he gave me permission. Next, his shirt came off in a cloud of buttons to let my fingers find the warm flesh beneath the fabric. Once my hands found his pants, Lucifer released me enough to pull off my own clothes.

We were a tangled frenzy of hands and mouths as each of us searched for more and more skin to touch, to kiss. The first time he slid into me, we didn't even make it to the bed. Lucifer bent me over the side of the couch and took me from behind, making the furniture creak with every movement.

"Jane, oh sweet, Jane," Lucifer grunted as he stroked a hand down my back. He pressed a kiss to my spine which made me shiver. "I will never get enough of being here, inside of you."

I hated how my mind immediately made me think he was saying goodbye. That he too thought our time was limited and wanted to get as much time in with me as possible. I didn't verbalize my thoughts. I feared they would become reality if I so much as hinted at it.

We came together there on the couch, gasping and panting for breath. Then Lucifer laid me on the bed and went back to the kitchen. He then grabbed the rest of the cheesecake and brought it back over to me, feeding me like a child each tiny bit at a time and kissing me in between each bite, never once taking any for himself.

"Good?" Lucifer asked after I had finished the last bite.

I hummed through my full mouth and nodded, lazily staring up at him. "Yes, thank you. You didn't want any?" I gestured to the empty container he sat on the floor by the bed.

"Oh, no. I had more fun watching you eat it than eating it myself. Besides," his fingers slid between my legs where I laid on my side and urged them open, "I have other plans that require you at full strength."

His hand pressed against my core, and I cried

out, thrusting my hips against his touch. His finger swirled around my clit before dipping inside of me to tease me there as well. After a moment, he shifted closer to me on the bed, so that he was pressed up against my back while I still stayed on my side.

The hard press of his cock rubbed my ass as he continued to torture me with his fingers. The hand not preoccupied lined his cock up with my center, and he thrust inside of me. Crying out, I pushed back letting him sink all the way in. The hand not between my legs grabbed the back of my neck holding me in place while he quickened his pace, moving harder and faster until I barely could breathe through the pleasure of it.

"Why am I not surprised to find you here? You know we have yet to find Uriel." Michael's irritated voice broke through the fog of pleasure and made me lift my head from my pillow briefly.

Lucifer lunged forward harder as he ignored his brother. And I did too, voluntarily or not, as I gasped, squeezing my eyes shut tight. The Devil's chuckle rumbled through my backside and into my core, and I groaned.

Hauling me up from the bed, Lucifer moved his hand from the back of my neck to the front of my throat and growled into my ear, "What better way to protect Jane than from deep inside of her?"

Fucking amen to that.

"Still, you can't very well protect her while you are otherwise occupied," Michael continued, much to my dismay. "What if Uriel attacked now? What would you do?"

"The same I'm going to say to you, either join in or shut the fuck up," I moaned out as Lucifer chuckled.

"So, brother," Lucifer purred as he slowed his pace briefly. "Which is it going to be?"

With a roll of his eyes, Michael shook his head and disappeared.

"Pity," I sighed, staring at where Michael had stood. "I'd have liked to try out both of you at once."

Lucifer let out a low growl and thrust hard. "Well, then my eager little human, let me see what I can do about making you forget about your disappointment."

And he did make me forget about it. All night long.

14

When I woke up the next morning, Lucifer was gone. A sense of loss filled my heart. I wondered if it would be a regular occurrence for us, going to bed together and waking up alone.

My eyes burned, and my throat tightened with emotion.

Fuck me. Get a grip.

I shook my head and swiped a hand over my eyes. I forced myself to get out of my warm comfy bed and walked to the kitchen. Turning on the coffee pot, I let it brew and headed for the bathroom.

I took my time in the shower and let the warm

water wash away the night and my anxiety of what the future may bring.

I shouldn't be worrying about the future anyway. I had a case that needed to be solved, and I was nowhere closer to solving it than I was yesterday. Going over what I'd learned so far, I tried to piece together what I might have missed.

The safe was moved, that was obvious. So, the person had to have the strength to move it. Then they had to be able to reset the safe with the new PIN. Who would know the PIN number though? If the safe belonged to the Civic Center, then I supposed they would know the PIN number as well, but why would one of them steal it?

It's worth a fortune, duh.

Well, besides the money. I mean, if I were the owners, I wouldn't want to lose a client like Andre who was spending tons of money to use their venue.

So, not the owners.

Maybe one of the assistants? We already knew Noah was a creep. He was going to sell the judges' names to one of the contestants. Too bad we didn't know who it was. I should check with Mandy to see if she ever got a hit on that phone number.

Turning off the water, I climbed out of the tub. As the shivers came on, I grabbed a towel, quickly dried off, and headed for some much-needed coffee. I went to the fridge and grabbed my creamer before pouring a cup of coffee and mixing it in. Taking a generous sip of it, I sighed. That's the stuff. Now, what else did I know?

Noah claimed he didn't steal the trophy, but could I really trust him not to lie? Lucifer said he was telling the truth, but he might know more than he was letting on.

Then there was Patrice. Klutzy, stammering, Patrice.

Could be an act? If she made herself look defenseless, people wouldn't think twice about her doing something so criminal. It would be my go-to if I wanted to get away with something. However, I wouldn't be stupid enough to keep working there.

The Shining twins were definitely on my list of suspects. Okay, so they only made it because I didn't like them, but it was my list, I could put who I wanted on it.

I hated to put Marco or Lisa on the list, they seemed really nice. Made me look fabulous too. However, I had to be fair. At least, until I could get their alibis.

The only ones I hadn't talked to were the contestants. And that was something I was really not looking forward too. If there was that much attitude in just the helpers, then I couldn't imagine the 'tude I was going to get when I start poking my nose in their business.

Guess I better get ready and stop procrastinating.

Instead of choosing something comfortable, I decided to look the part. Maybe the contestants would be more likely to talk to me if I looked like one of them. Pulling on a pair of skinny jeans, I grabbed my favorite red heels and then hunted around the apartment for a top. Now, what said fashionista in training?

After a few minutes of searching, I realized my clothes sucked. The only thing I had was the shirt from yesterday, and I so wasn't going to get caught wearing the same thing two days in a row. I'd never hear the end of it from the twins.

"She doesn't look like much?" a voice I didn't know made me freeze. I pretended to keep searching for a top while out of the side of my eye, I caught sight of my two stalkers.

"I don't know, Azrael. She does have something about her." The tone of his voice made me think he was staring at some of my more private parts.

Tempted to cover myself and kick them out, I had to keep up the pretense that I couldn't see them. If I couldn't see them then they would get bored and leave, or at least that was the theory.

"Well, obviously, there has to be something about her that has made the mighty Michael neglect his duties?" The one called Azrael cocked his head, making his long white hair fall over his shoulder. The clothing they picked out looked like they had taken right off a billboard. They were definitely runway model style in their open neck shirts and tight jeans. "What do you think, Raphael? Do you think she is worth it?"

"Well, she obviously can't see us or she'd have tattled to her bodyguards about us already." Raphael walked over to me and knelt by my feet, his bright green eyes boring into me. He reached a hand out and tried to touch me, but his hand went right through my stomach and made my body flinch from the buzzing. "I want to know how she makes them solid. And why she can't see us?"

"Maybe they lied." Azrael crossed his arms over his chest and moved closer. "Lucifer is one of the ones who claims to have been spending time with her." His nose crinkled. "Do you think they are really fornicating with this ape? How... vulgar."

Raphael laughed. "Come now, don't act like you haven't watched the humans and wondered what all the fuss was about. If you had a chance to put your dick in someone, you would, even taking second or in this case third go at her."

That was it. I couldn't stand listening to them talk about me like I was a piece of meat they could use and get rid of.

I jerked up and spun around my hands on my hips, glaring at the two of them. "I don't care who you think you are, but you're not getting anywhere near my bits. So, you can just take your over ego'd, self-righteous ass and go back to Heaven with the rest of them."

"Ah, so you can see us." Azrael stroked his chin, his eyes alight with delight. "I was wondering if you were just pretending."

"Yeah, well, you aren't that fascinating. It wasn't that hard to ignore you." I rolled my eyes and grabbed a random t-shirt, no longer able to stand them staring at my tits.

"Oh, I can see why they like you so much." Raphael snorted and poked a finger at my chest. "You have sass. Tell me," he leaned forward and put his face right in front of mine, "does that sass transfer to the bedroom?" He gestured to the bed with his head.

"Fuck you," I snarled.

"Gladly, just tell me how you made them corporeal, and I'd be happy to find out what all the fuss is about." He trailed his finger across my chest in an annoyingly buzzing trail.

"Well, get used to disappointment." I jerked my arm through his in an attempt to knock him away. When he only laughed and continued trying to touch me, I shook my head and moved away from him. "I've got things to do, and none of those include adding two more angels to my roster. And if I did, they would certainly never be you."

"Never is a long time, Jane Mehr." Azrael moved closer to me, his eyes on me as he searched my face for something. "You might find yourself singing a different tune at some point. We can provide you with far greater protection than any of them can."

I laughed. "You think you're better than two of God's most powerful angels and the Devil? I doubt that."

"Things are changing all the time." Azrael stopped before me. "Especially in Heaven. Power shifts. Favorites change. Right now, your playthings aren't getting a lot of praise for fraternizing with a human."

What Azrael said made me pause. I already

knew that those in Heaven weren't happy with my guys being with me. However, I didn't know how bad. The guys hadn't really kept me in that loop.

Now, it was going to bite them in the ass.

Sighing, I dragged a hand through my still wet hair and almost called out to the others to come help me. I was stopped by my ringing phone. Saved by the bell.

Turning away from them, I reached for my phone. "Yeah?" I answered.

"Don't sound to so excited," Mandy said dryly. "Geez, it's not like I'm your best friend or anything."

Glancing behind me, I was happy to see the two intruders had taken the hint and took off. I just wondered for how long.

"Sorry," I grumbled. "Just depressed about the boring disaster that has become my closest." I certainly wasn't going to tell Mandy they had showed up. It would only make her worry.

"Huh?"

I cupped my elbow with my hand and leaned into the phone. "I don't have anything to wear that will make some fashion designers want to talk to me like I'm one of them."

"You're not one of them though," Mandy pointed out unhelpfully.

"Well, no duh. They don't need to know that." I dug through my pile of laundry I never got around to putting up, hoping against hope that some magical elves had left me something overnight.

"What about that blouse?" Mandy suggested.

"What blouse?" I grunted as I struggled to stand back up on my heels.

"You know, that one with the built-in push up bra. You wore it at that club when you were trying to get us free drinks."

I let out a laugh. "Oh, yeah. If I do recall, that shirt worked like a charm. We didn't pay for anything that night and never had a dry moment."

Mandy snorted. "Speak for yourself."

Laughing once more, I moved from my living room area to the closet. Opening it was a hazard, and I rarely used anything in it because of the avalanche that came pouring out the moment I opened it. Hiding behind the door as I pulled it open, I watched with a bit of a grimace as shoes, books, and whatnot tumbled out of the closet. I really needed to go through this crap.

You said that last time you opened it. It's why we don't use anything in it unless it's an emergency.

Well, today counted as an emergency.

"What was that?" Mandy asked.

"Uh, nothing," I reassured her as I stepped over the pile on the floor, almost face planting when my heel caught on something.

"You haven't cleaned your closet yet, have you?"

"I don't like your tone."

Mandy sighed. I could hear the disapproval in her voice which meant she was probably tugging on her ponytail too. "It's no wonder you never find anything in that mess. You're going to break a leg one of these days, too, or maybe the weight of it all will fall through to the lower level."

I giggled. "Nah, you're exaggerating." Well, I hoped she was. "Anyway, I don't have time to clean. I have a business to run and hot angels to bang."

"You could get one of those angels to clean your closet," she pointed out.

A vivid image of the guys dressed up in butler outfits cleaning my house flashed into my mind, and a body wracking shiver ran through me. Yes, please. "If they're going to clean anything, it would be the mess in my panties, not my closet."

"Gross." Mandy made a gagging noise. "Where

are your angels? Aren't they usually hovering nearby?"

I let out a long breath as I tried to hide my recent fears. "Uh, yeah. Not right now. They had some emergency or something." At least, I hoped that was it. I'd hate to think something had happened to them. Lately, they never left me alone. So, if I was by myself, then it only means something bad happened.

"What's wrong?"

"You know, sometimes it sucks having a best friend who knows me so well. Sometimes I wanna wallow in my own crap for once," I told her though I didn't really mean it. I found the shirt in question from my closet and pulled it off the hanger. I then attempted to close the closet and gave up promptly. I'd deal with it later.

"No, you don't," Mandy echoed my thoughts. "You need someone to vent to, or you'd go crazy. So, what's wrong? Are they giving you a hard time?"

"Not much of any time actually." I sighed and sank down onto the kitchen chair. I didn't want to bring Mandy into this crap, but she was asking for it, and what kind of friend would I be if I didn't deliver? "There's been a development."

"What kind of development?" The suspicion in her voice reminded me that she was a cop. She was probably already prepared to shoot someone, even an angel, for me if it came down to it.

Taking my bra off, I struggled into my new shirt, only half noticing how nice the girls looked in this top. What a waste of boobage. I wouldn't get laid or free drinks today.

"Jane?" Mandy reminded me she was waiting for an answer.

"You shouldn't worry about it," I said as I tried to sound as nonchalant as possible. "You can't do anything about it anyway. The guys are taking care of it."

"But there is something though?"

"Apparently, the other angels aren't happy with our relationship and want to stop it." I didn't include the part where they didn't care if that meant killing me. Mandy would freak the fuck out.

"That's understandable."

"What now?" I stood up suddenly, not happy with her easy agreement. "I don't want to stop it."

"But Jane," Mandy replied with that tone of voice that said she was going to lecture me, "they're angels. You're a human. How exactly did you think this was going to end? You're going to die eventually, and as far as you know, they live forever."

I hated that she was verbalizing all the worries I'd had recently. It made them so much more real. "I know that… which is why I should get in all the time I can with them now before they leave me."

Mandy was quiet for a moment and then asked in a cautious voice. "Jane, are you in love with them?"

"Maybe." Swallowing thickly, I moved to the kitchen and grabbed my coffee cup. I needed the caffeine, feelings were hard work.

"Then there's nothing I can do to help you," Mandy relented. "Physically, I'll kick their asses if they hurt you. But emotionally? I can only tell you to be careful, but it seems like you already let yourself get attached. So, just let me know when to come with the wine and ice cream."

I nodded, my emotions too thick to speak, then I remembered she couldn't see me. "Yeah," I croaked after I cleared my throat. "I will. Thanks." Before Mandy could hang up, I remembered I needed to talk to her. "Oh, hey, did you trace that call yet?"

"What am I magic?" Mandy laughed. "I submitted the request for a trace, but they haven't gotten back to me yet. My favors only extend so far. I'll have something when I have something."

"Well, if you'd use your God-given gifts you'd get a lot further," I reminded her as I grabbed my purse and headed for the door.

Mandy laughed. "Whatever. I have to get back to work before O'Connor catches me slacking."

"Alright, if you must. Give him hell," I told her before hanging up the phone and leaving my apartment. I hurried into my car and toward the Civic Center. I half expected one of the guys to show up, but none of them did. That put me in a sour mood by the time I pulled into the Civic Center's parking lot.

"Name?" the guard asked, barely giving me a glance.

Irritation flooded me. "Jane Mehr. I was here yesterday."

"No one gets in unless they're on the list." The guard scanned the list and then reluctantly found my name. "Go ahead."

Marching past the guard, I searched the arena for a familiar face. When I caught sight of the cotton-candy-haired stylist, I headed her way. "Lisa. Hey."

Lisa glanced up from the model she was

working on. When she caught sight of me, her lips slid into a crooked smile. "Well, I be damned. Look who's back. You coming to get another makeover?"

I shook my head and offered her a small smile in return. "Nah, I'm good. I was going to go around and talk to some of the designers today. Want to point them out to me?"

Sticking a couple of pins in the hair of the girl she was working on, Lisa turned slightly. "Uh, yeah." She tapped her lip with the end of her comb and looked around. "Ah! There. See that one?" She pointed out a woman with dark skin and bright red hair. Currently, she was in the middle of ripping a new ass hole into a guy with long white hair. He had a thin face and sharp nose that he held high in the air even as the woman yelled at him.

"Yeah?"

"That's Kesha, and the guy she is bitching out is Jean Claude. He's French." She gave the model she was working on an oo-la-la gesture, making her giggle. "They're both contestants, but good luck getting a word in edgewise, girl."

I nodded with a grimace. "Thanks, I'll start there."

The yelling got louder as I approached the two of them, and it didn't make me feel any better about having to talk to them without my hot angels as a buffer. They always made everything just a bit more bearable.

"I do not care about your bitching!" Jean Claude waved Kesha off in a high-pitched French accent. The accent was so over the top that I had doubts that it was real. "I am not… how do you say… your whipping boy."

"Fuck off, you over-powdered pretty boy." Kesha shoved her long nails into Jean Claude's chest. "I'm not going to sit here and let you—"

"Excuse me." I tried to interrupt which earned me a collective 'what?' when both heads swiveled in my direction. "Hi, I'm Jane. Andre has been letting me poke around." I shifted in place, putting a hand on my hip and trying to look cool and confident. Under their tight scrutiny I was anything but.

"Well, poke around elsewhere. I'm busy." Kesha waved me off, flipped Jean Claude off, then gave me her back.

"If you'll just give me a second to ask a few questions—" I called after the fiery redhead.

"Do not bother with her." Jean Claude barked a laugh as he took my hand in his hand. He brushed his lips against the back of my hand, and I cringed. "She is a frigid bitch."

Jerking my hand away from him, I didn't bother hiding my disgust as I rubbed my hand on my pants. "Yeah. Okay. I still need to talk to her. And you... unfortunately. Where were you this weekend?"

"Why?" Kesha snapped as she turned back to me.

Crap. I hadn't thought of a reason to ask for their alibis. Quick, Jane. Think of something.

"Andre wants to be sure no one is talking to the press about the contest yet." I tried not to sag as I spit out my excuse.

Kesha shook her head with a snort. "Whatever. The bossman is a real piece of work. Too tightly wound if you know what I mean." She quirked a brow as her lips curled up at the edges. I got her meaning.

"So?" I urged on.

"I was at my shop. Ask my half a dozen assistant and designers." She waved her hand around the area. "Most of us are working our asses off to be here. We're not playing at winning."

"And you?" I glanced to the French douchebag. "Were you working?"

Jean Claude threw his head back and laughed, flipping his hair over his shoulder. "No, you Americans are all work and no play. Jean Claude was at the Blessed Falls Spa and Resort. Call them. They will tell you." He wiggled his fingers at me like I was supposed to hop to it.

"Uh, okay. Thanks. Can you point me in the direction of the others…?" I trailed off, looking around for someone else that might be a contestant.

Jean Claude made an annoyed sound. "Eh… Marsha is probably up Andre's backside. So, I'd check there. And Antoine…?" He looked toward Kesha, who only seemed mildly interested any more. "Probably out back fucking the help." They both laughed at that.

Trying to hide how disgusted I felt, I left the two of them to find my next target.

Thankfully, I found Marsha exactly where they said she'd be… with Andre.

The only way I could describe Marsha was doll-like. She wore a bright teal dress and black-rimmed glasses. Her dirty blonde hair fell down her back in curls, and she had a giggle that reminded me of bells. I wondered if she practiced it in the mirror.

"Oh, Andre," she cooed as she placed a hand on his arm. "You are too funny."

Andre brushed her compliment aside and

pointed toward the office. "I've got to head back in. Let me know if you have any more trouble."

When Andre saw me approaching, he paused his escape and offered me a small smile and a wave. I waved back, my smile a bit forced. Marsha turned around to look at who Andre was waving to.

"Hello, Marsha. I'm Jane." I offered her my hand, and she took it reluctantly. "I'm just checking in with all the designers to make sure we're keeping things close to the chest about the competition." She cocked her head to the side, her brows furrowed. Great. A dumb one. "I need to know where you were this weekend. For security reasons."

This got a reaction. Marsha's face turned beet red, and a hand went to her face in surprise. "Why would you need to know that?" she stuttered, really playing up the innocence act.

I tried to calm her fears. "We just want to be sure no one is leaking anyone else's work to the press. So…?"

Marsha ducked her head and then muttered something I didn't catch.

"What was that?" I angled my head toward her and put my hand behind my ear. "I didn't quite hear you."

She leaned forward and murmured, "I was with my master all weekend."

My face scrunched in confusion. "Your master?"

Marsha shifted from one foot to the other and got even more embarrassed. "You know... my master," she repeated in an effort to get me to understand what she was saying, and I still wasn't getting it.

"You mean like your boss?"

With a huff and a stomp of her foot, she pulled out her phone and typed something in. Then she shoved it in my face. The site she brought up was a **BDSM** website showing women and men in compromising positions, some of them bound and others kneeling. All of them looked more than happy to be there.

"Oh. Oh." I gaped at the page and then felt my own face flush. "Okay. Thank you. I'll write that... you were busy." That got a relieved expression from her.

"That would be appreciated." Marsha nodded and then looked around. "Can I go?"

"Yeah. Go ahead." Geez. Some strange characters they had here, and there were still more on my list.

15

F inding Tony was trickier than the others. I searched around the arena for someone who would look like a Tony but to no avail. Then I remembered Jean Claude had mentioned Tony would be out back, hopefully not screwing someone.

Out by the loading docks still packed with delivery trucks, I continued my search. I found Patrice before I found Tony. The small assistant stood bent at the waist, breathing into a paper bag.

"Patrice?" I placed a hand on her shoulder. "Are you alright?"

Startled by my gentle touch, Patrice jerked away from me as the bag fell from her mouth. "Uh, Jane, right?"

"Yeah." I offered her a small smile, then gestured to the bag. "Hard day?"

Patrice scoffed. "You could say that. I love assisting Andre but these designers…" She shook her head and frowned. "They're—"

I watched her struggle for the word, but I think she was just too polite to say what was really on her mind, so I helped her out. "Big pains in the ass."

She let out a hard laugh. "Yeah. The biggest."

"You know," I mused, "I don't know if I could offer you the same pay as Andre, but if you ever need another job, I could always use an assistant."

"Oh?" Patrice arched a brow.

I pulled my card out and handed it to her.

"Gotcha! Psychic Detective Agency?" Her brows scrunched together behind her large rimmed glasses. "But I thought you were interested in the fashion industry?"

I chuckled. "You're smarter than that Patrice." I gestured at our clothes. "You dress better than me."

"You did seem a bit out of place." Patrice grinned and tucked the card into her planner on the floor. "So does Andre know you're…?" She waved a hand at me.

"Psychic? Yeah, he hired me, but don't tell him that." I winked and held a finger up. "It's a secret."

"For the missing trophy, right?"

I pulled back, surprise clearly on my face. "How did you know about that? Andre said he'd kept it hush-hush."

Patrice smirked and adjusted her glasses as she picked up her things. "Andre couldn't tie his own shoe without me, and like you said, I'm smarter than that." I gave her a curious but impressed look. "I knew something was going on the moment he wouldn't let anyone else into the office. He even kept Marsha... anyway, have you found it yet?"

I had a feeling she wanted to say more about Marsha, the doll-like designer who couldn't stay away from Andre. I wondered if she actually liked the sexy billionaire or if she was hoping to get in good with the boss?

Shaking my head, I sighed. "No, not yet. You don't have any clues, do you?"

Patrice tapped her chin and then shook her head. "I wish I could say I knew. Have you tried talking to the designers?"

"Just did, well, except for those who dropped out." I paused and looked around. "And Tony who I can't seem to find."

"Oh." Patrice's eyes lit up. "He's talking up the

delivery gal." She pointed her thumb over her shoulder with an eye roll.

"And by talking up, you mean…?" I trailed off and did a hip thrust which made Patrice giggle.

"Yeah, exactly. So be warned. You may get scarred for life." She grinned, and we shared another laugh.

"Thanks, and don't forget to hit me up." I pointed at her planner where she'd put my card. "Being a detective is so much more fun than…" I waved a hand around. "… this."

Patrice smiled and nodded. "I'll keep that in mind. Thank you."

With a goodbye wave, I headed toward the truck she said Tony was at with a bit more pep in my step… until the truck started to shift back and forward. My steps slowed as my ears caught the distinct sounds of someone having a far too good of a time on the clock.

Knowing I was stupid for even doing it, I rounded the corner and found my missing designer balls deep inside a cut brunette. He had her pressed up against the side of the truck, her face smashed against the metal siding. She wasn't complaining though, not with the way she was moaning and jerking her hips back toward him.

Rather than interrupt them, I backed away, spun on my heel, and almost ran right through an incorporeal Michael. "Woah, sneak up on a girl, why don't you?"

Michael didn't laugh or show any indication that he had heard me. In fact, at closer inspection, he hardly seemed there at all. His brows were furrowed, and his eyes filled with an intense emotion I'd never seen before.

"What's wrong?"

Michael wouldn't look at me, that emotion on his face becoming darker by the second. I tried to grab him and then cursed when my hands went through him. Sometimes I hated this, not being able to touch them. With a sigh of frustration, I pulled my pin from my shirt and winced as I pricked my finger. That was getting old too.

"Here." I held my finger up to him, but he didn't even glance at it. "Michael, take the damn blood already."

His pale blue eyes jerked to me finally. They locked onto mine, and for a moment, I thought he didn't see me. Then his eyes shifted to the blood. He pressed his mouth to my finger, only touching me long enough to take the blood. Once he was corporeal, I clamped my hands on the side of his face and pulled him down to my level.

"There's my guy," I murmured, pressing my forehead against the warmth of his brow. I brushed our noses together and then kissed him softly. Michael let me do all of this almost mechanically, never stopping me but not encouraging me either. When I pulled back, I searched his gaze. "What's wrong?"

Michael placed his hand on top of mine and shook his head. "I'm fine. Do not worry for me."

I scoffed. "Of course, I worry for you. For all of you."

"It's Heavenly business. It is none of your concern."

I pulled back from him, getting pissed off. "None of my concern?" I laughed bitterly. "Everything to do with you and Heaven became my concern when you wouldn't leave me alone, so don't think that you can ice me out now because I'm a lowly human."

"Jane?" Michael tried to reach for me, but I pulled away.

"No!" I raised my voice as I shook my head. "You know, you think you're invincible, but you wouldn't be so worried about Uriel if you didn't think you could get hurt. So, excuse me for giving a damn."

Michael let out a frustrated growl. "But you shouldn't feel that way about us. That's what has caused this whole problem because we all got too involved. We forgot what we are." His voice lowered as he moved closer to me. "Because we became so consumed by you."

I let him take my hands and draw me closer, and I tried to push down my emotions to meet his gaze. "Are you leaving me?"

Instead of answering, he moved away and looked around. "How is the case going? Have you found the culprit?"

Frowning, I started to ask him why he was deflecting but decided against it. "Not yet. I'm working on it."

Michael was quiet for a moment and then, out of the blue, he said, "Let's go get some ice cream."

Not sure where the sudden urge for frozen sugar came from, but I wasn't going to argue. Today was just one of those days. I was still holding out hopes that he would talk to me. Tell me what was really going on, for once.

We got in my car and drove to my favorite frozen yogurt place.

Okay, so it wasn't ice cream, but it was near the same thing. The Tasty Orange was one of my favorite places in town. When I was upset, it was the place I went to. The screaming orange and white decorations, the vinyl seats, and the strong scent of sweets filled the air.

"Why don't you find us a seat?" I nodded toward the booths lining the walls. "I'll grab us something to eat."

Michael glanced at the yogurt dispensers and then to the condiments. "I think I would like to try it myself." He moved toward the dispensers, walking slowly down the aisle as he read each flavor.

Curious to see how he would handle it, I grabbed us a couple of bowls and handed him one. "Here. Put it in this."

Michael tilted his head toward me and took the bowl. Then he moved to one of the dispensers, put his bowl beneath it, and pulled the handle.

"Apple pie, bold choice." I moved up next to him, my lips tilting up at the edges. "I'm more into the classics, to be honest." Putting my cup underneath the dispenser for vanilla, I filled my bowl with a generous amount before moving to the strawberry one.

"I've always wanted to know what it tastes like," Michael said, staring down at the bowl in his hand.

I snorted. "Well, I can tell you." I dipped my spoon into his bowl and popped a spoonful into my mouth. "It's never as good as the real thing." I hummed and then moved back to filling my bowl up. "Now, real apple pie is warm and gooey on the inside, the crust is just the right amount of crumbly. Oh! And with vanilla ice cream on top." I winked and grinned at him before moving to the condiments.

"And which of these should I add?" Michael asked.

I clucked my tongue and scanned the toppings. What would go best with apple pie? "Fruits, obviously." I pointed at the chopped-up strawberries and cherries, watching as Michael scooped large spoonfuls into his bowl. "And if you want to get really daring you could mix it up and go with something more contrasting. Like gummies." I stuck my fingers into the container and popped one of the gummie worms into my mouth.

"Ma'am, stop eating before you pay," the teenage girl behind the counter snapped at me and then saw Michael. Her mouth fell open a bit, and if it were a cartoon, her tongue would have unraveled onto the floor, and her heart would have beat out of her chest.

"Sorry." I grinned, turned to Michael, and asked, "So, what's it going to be?"

Those gorgeous blue eyes scanned the counter, his lips pressed tightly into a firm line. He made every decision so seriously, with such calculation. It made the fact that he even got involved with me in the first place so surprising.

After a moment or so, he reached for the chocolate chips and then the strawberries. Lastly, he topped it off with some gummie bears.

I smirked. "Go big or go home, I always say."

He didn't smile back but brought his bowl over to the cashier with me. I gestured for him to place it on the scale and then paid the cashier when she was done weighing both of our yogurt concoctions.

"Thanks." I took my debit card back, smiling at how starstruck the teenager was. If it had been an old lady, she'd still ogle Michael. He was just that attractive. Well, it wasn't really the looks that made people gape. It was the ethereal otherworldliness about him that had people stopping and staring.

We took a seat in one of the near booths. After we sat across from each other, I took a small bite of my yogurt as I watched him. He scooped a spoonful and brought it to his mouth. Parting his lips, he slid the spoon into his mouth.

My lips ticked up at the edges. "Good?"

His brows furrowed, and then as he moved the yogurt around in his mouth, those brows lifted. "Yes. It is an interesting flavor. Sweet and yet…" His jaws worked the mouthful. "Chewy."

I giggled. "That's the gummies. Maybe next time you could pick something simpler."

Arching a brow, Michael locked eyes with me. "I have been called many things, but simple is not one of them."

I grinned as I moved my spoon around in my bowl. "No, I wouldn't call you that."

"So, what have you learned on the case?"

Taking another bite of my yogurt, I mulled over his question. "I've talked to all the contestants at the Civic Center." I paused and grimaced slightly at the image of Tony going at it. "Well, most of them. There are a couple who've dropped out. I was just about to go hunt them down when you showed up."

Michael didn't answer that but quietly ate his treat. I watched him with growing curiosity and frustration. What was he doing here? What were they doing when they left me? They dropped in and out of my life at random without a word about any of it. They just keep thinking that I was going to be fine being in the dark. Well, I was done with that. It was time for some answers.

"Not now, Jane." Michael's firm but commanding voice made whatever I was going to say freeze on my lips. "Can I just be here… with you?"

There was a need there in his words, in the pinched skin around his eyes that made me pause. It was similar to the look Lucifer had given me. There was something they weren't telling me… but I could wait for now. What Michael needed wasn't me questioning him right now, that much I could tell in that need.

"Alright, so want to come with me to interrogate some crazies?" I popped my spoon into my mouth and grinned around it.

Michael took the spoon from my mouth before scooping it into my bowl.

"Hey!" I reached out to take my spoon back. He was too quick for me though. "That was mine."

Michael hummed around my spoon and then handed it back to me. "I think I could learn to live with simple." The way he said it brought heat to my cheeks, and I realized he was not talking about the frozen yogurt anymore.

16

I drove to the address Andre texted me for one of the dropouts, a man named Oliver Quid. He lived close to my side of town which hopefully meant he would be less of a pain in the ass than the others.

Wishful thinking, I know.

Parking the car, Michael and I walked up to the yellow house with a mini windmill in the front lawn and a flamingo giving me the evil eye. It was not a promising start.

"Let me do the talking," I told Michael as I pushed the doorbell. "I don't want an alpha male pissing contest. I want information, not black eyes and closed lips."

"I believe you have me mistaken with someone

else." Michael crossed his arms over his chest and stared menacingly at the closed door.

"See? That look right there." I pointed at his face, then lowered my voice as I heard someone moving around inside. "That's not helping."

Michael sighed and dropped his arms. "How would you like me to look?"

"Approachable." I barely got the word out before the front door opened to reveal a slender guy with a buzzed haircut and blue rimmed circle glasses. His orange button up shirt could be seen beneath his royal purple sweater, a combination that made even me flinch. He held a tissue to his nose as he sniffed, pulling my attention to his red-rimmed eyes.

"What do you want?" Oliver asked as his eyes narrowed on me, but then they slid over to Michael. Flustered by the angel, Oliver brought his tissue to his nose and tried to look less of a mess. "I'm sorry for my appearance, I've been having a bad week. My boyfriend just broke up with me."

Smooth. I rolled my eyes. Very smooth.

"I'm Jane." I stepped closer, trying to draw his eyes off Michael and onto me. "Andre sent me from the contest? You're Oliver?"

Oliver reluctantly looked at me, but it wasn't a

nice look. "What does he want? I already told him I quit, and I didn't need the entry fee back."

I nodded. "Yes, I know, but we're just trying to get a list of where everyone was this weekend. We've had a bit of a press leak and are trying to figure out where it might have gone wrong."

The designer's shoulders sagged, and he backed away from the door. "Come inside, I suppose. You never know who's listening around here." He glanced around the doorway like paparazzi were going to jump out at any moment.

Michael and I exchanged a look before we followed the man inside. While Michael was busy looking for things that might stick out, I noticed the pictures of the Oliver with another man. He was much younger looking than Oliver who looked to be in his late thirties. The other man was of Hispanic descent with a wily look in his eyes, like he knew that he was too hot for the older designer.

"Who's this?" I picked up the picture and showed Oliver. "The boyfriend?"

"Yes, that's Roger. He's my... Well, I guess he *was* my boyfriend." Oliver moved to the kitchen and held up a teapot. "Tea? It's green."

I waved him off, not rude enough to tell him how disgusting that crap was to me. Michael wasn't even paying us any mind. He was looking around the house, being his annoyingly observant self.

"You know, I never did used to like the stuff myself, but then Roger would have a cup every day." He huffed a laugh. "Said it would be good for my heart." He bowed his head and sniffed a bit.

I didn't want to kick a good guy while he was down, but some things couldn't wait. "So, not to be insensitive, but how did you and Oliver break up?"

Oliver lifted his head and dabbed his eyes. "Why does anyone break up?" He shrugged evasively as he went about making himself a cup of tea.

"Still, all the same. Did he happen to do it this last weekend?" I arched a brow, trying to get him to give me something to rule him out so I could get out of this house. I couldn't stand myself crying, let alone watching a grown man do the same.

As Oliver blew the steam away off his teacup, he nodded sadly. "Yes, we went away for the week-end. St. Bart's. I thought we were going to have a romantic weekend that would end with me propos-ing, but Roger had other thoughts." He let out a shaky laugh.

"Roger left you for someone else."

Oliver and I both turned to look at Michael

who paused at the desk in the open dining room. He held up a picture of Roger with another man, a more attractive one that was probably the same age as him.

"Put those back." Oliver sat his cup down and scurried over to the desk to hide the dozen pictures of Roger and the man in a dozen different places.

"That's quite a collection of photos," I commented as I moved over to them. "You know, when someone dumps me, I tend to get drunk and rock out in my underwear. Not," I gestured to the photos, "stalk him?"

"I'm not stalking him!" Oliver's voice screeched as he held the images to his chest. "I just wanted to check out the competition."

It was plain to me that Oliver was hoping to woo Roger back, and it was so sad how he thought that. I mean, when someone leaves you for someone better and, by the photos, someone they were seeing behind your back, the likelihood that you were going to get back together was close to nil.

I shot a look over at Michael. The tight frown on his lips said he agreed with me. Oliver was a little nutso.

"So, you were gone all weekend?" I reiterated, trying to get back on topic.

"Yes, yes. And then Roger broke up with me, and I've been home all week, it's why I dropped out," Oliver rushed to tell me but seemed far too nervous for me to believe him.

"Really?"

Michael added on to my question with, "You are not being entirely truthful."

Oliver's eyes widened, and he jumped back, his eyes darting to Michael. "What? Yes, I am."

"Tut-tut-tut." I waved a finger at Oliver. "My guy is pretty observant. If he thinks you're holding back on me, then I have to believe him. So, what is it, Oliver? I find it hard to believe that you quit the contest just because your boyfriend broke up with you for someone else." I crossed my arms over my chest and locked eyes with him.

"He was the love of my life," he stuttered as he backed away from us. "I couldn't sleep, let alone focus on winning."

I shook my head. "Likely story, they told me you guys prep all year for this contest. There's no way you'd give up the chance to become an award-winning designer for this. I mean, I have some hot boyfriends, but even I wouldn't let it ruin my life."

Michael gave me a strange look that I wanted to ask about but couldn't in front of Oliver.

"Fine, fine." Oliver huffed, holding his hands up. "I didn't quit because of Roger, though he did break up with me." He chucked the photos on the table. "And cheating on me, which is obvious. But I didn't back out because of him. Fucking twat." Oliver huffed. "I got a call a few weeks ago. Someone offering me ten grand to back out of the contest."

"Ten grand, that's quite a bit of money," I nodded along, explaining to Michael at the same time, "but isn't the reward for winning a crap ton more than that?"

"Oh, yeah." Oliver vigorously shook his head up and down. "That's why I blew them off."

"But not now?" I angled my head to the side. "What changed?"

Oliver moved past us to the wet bar in the dining room. Pouring himself a generous glass of what looked to be scotch, he took a large drink before answering. "They called back the day after Roger broke up with me and offered fifty thousand for me to quit."

"And you took it?"

Draining his glass, Oliver sucked on his teeth. "Yep. I was vulnerable and tired. I just wanted a break. That money would help me get the break I needed while I recalculated my life without Roger."

I gestured to the photos on the ground. "You mean, pay for your private detective?"

Oliver scowled at me. "That too."

"Did they pay you?"

My head jerked to Michael, happy he thought to ask. "Yeah. Did they?"

"Of course. After I called Andre, they texted me from an unknown number and told me the funds had been deposited. I didn't even know how they got my account number, but the money was there, so I wasn't going to ask questions." Oliver poured another glass and sat down on the nearest seat, his shoulder curling forward as he slouched.

"Do you know who called you?" I tried, hoping against hope that we'd get a lead.

"No, like I said, the number was unknown or blocked, I guess." Oliver sighed heavily.

"Did you recognize the voice? Was it male or female?" I rushed through the questions, trying to get something out of this whole ordeal.

"Male, I think." Oliver pressed a hand to his forehead as if trying to force something out. "No one I recognized in any case. They didn't say who they were, just that they wanted me out. I guess I should be flattered they thought I was a big enough threat to them that they had to pay me off."

"Yeah, I guess. That's a good way to look at it." I gave Michael a look and jerked my head toward the door. We were done here. This guy couldn't tell us anything else, and unless I could track the account the money came from, doubtful, then I was no closer to who took the trophy. Apparently, though, someone wanted to win and badly.

"Well, Oliver," I smacked my lips, "thank you for your time. I'll be sure to keep this hush-hush." I zipped my lips and nodded. "Mum's the word."

"I appreciate it." Oliver inclined his head, not getting up to walk us out.

I led Michael back through the house and out the front door, where I stopped in my tracks. There, standing in the middle of Oliver's front yard, was Uriel.

Great, just what my day needed.

17

"What are you doing here?" Michael's voice boomed through the neighborhood while I quickly checked to see if he had shut the front door. The last thing we needed was for some drama queen designer coming out here to be cannon fodder.

Thankfully, the door was shut and probably locked for good measure. So, the only thing I had to worry about was pedestrians going by. So far, none of them thought anything was out of the ordinary, but Michael and Uriel were just getting started.

"I'm here to make you come back, brother." Uriel's arms crossed over each other, a tight frown on his lips. He wore the same outdated Biblical rope dress thing, really, I don't know what it's called nor wanted to, and left his black hair down hanging around his face. It would be a nice face too if he smiled instead of glared at everyone.

"You are not the commander of me." Michael took the few steps down from Oliver's front porch to approach the domineering angel. "I am the leader of God's armies, his right hand. No one but our father tells me what to do."

I cleared my throat and gave him a side eye. Michael didn't bother acknowledging my hint. Freaking men.

"That was then, Michael, before you got involved with her." Uriel pointed a finger at me, like I was something he had stepped on and had to scrape off his shoe. "Until you let go of your human pet, no one will take orders from you."

I scoffed. "Excuse me." I waved a hand in the air which drew Uriel's gaze to me. "I am no one's pet. I make my own decisions and can take care of myself. If anyone has pets, it's me. Three large ones that have been nothing but pains in my ass since day one."

I shot a look to Michael who was staring at me like he wanted me to shut up. Too damn bad.

As I moved away from Michael, I locked my eyes

on Uriel, hoping that my face said bad ass bitch, but with my luck, I probably just looked constipated. "In fact, you're becoming one of those pains with the way you keep popping up everywhere unannounced. You have been worse for my love life than that perm I had back in high school." I so wasn't going into detail on that, it was not one of my better years.

"You are but a bug in the grand—" Uriel tried to scoff.

"Yeah, yeah," I cut him off, holding my hands out to my sides. "So you've said, but what are you really bitching about, huh?" I cocked my head to the side as I studied Uriel's face. "Are you jealous? Is that it? Because if you're wanting a piece of this, then you're out of luck. I am over my quota on incorporeal boyfriends. I have enough to handle with the ones I have."

"I would not lower myself to lie with filth such as you," Uriel spit out, dropping his hands to his side as his fingers curled into fists.

"Ouch," I said with mock pain, pretending he had hit me in the chest. "You really know how to kill a girl's self-esteem."

Michael snorted. "Like you don't have plenty."

I glanced back at the archangel and arched a

brow. "Are we helping or hurting? Ask that when you open your mouth."

"You're one to talk," Michael retorted with a smirk. "You couldn't keep yourself out of trouble for five minutes, even without angels on your trail."

I shrugged. "What can I say danger just loves me." I beamed back at him and then turned back to Uriel who was simply staring daggers at the both of us. "Now, where was I? Oh yeah. I'm a bug, huh? Well, I think this is a case of the angel protesth too much. Why don't you try out what the others are so hard core on getting, instead of making your snap judgments?" I pulled the pin from my shirt and pricked my finger before holding it out to him. "Here it is, I'm offering it freely to you."

For a second, I thought Uriel might actually go for it, but then his nose scrunched up and a blast of disgust covered his face. "I would never put any part of you in my body."

I shrugged and popped the finger into my mouth, cleaning off the blood before turning to Michael. "Can't say I didn't try?"

Michael let out an exasperated sigh before reaching out to grab my elbow and pull me back to his side. I let out a yelp but went with him. Because

I wanted to, not because he made me, let's get that clear.

"Michael, while you dally with this human, your soldiers are becoming restless," Uriel proclaimed like, well, an angel from on high. "They question why their commander isn't in Heaven. What are we to tell them? Would they think you still an all-powerful archangel if they knew that you spend your hours with this ape?" His eyes flashed with anger and condescension towards me.

I glanced between Michael and Uriel, wondering what Michael would do. A part of me hoped he would put the little bugger in his place, that he'd say I love Jane and I'm staying her with her so you can just fuck right off.

But that was not what he said.

Michael's jaw tightened, and then, after a moment, he released all tension from his body and turned to me. Cupping my cheek with his hand, he lowered his face down to mine. "I do need to go. Not because of what he said, but because there are others who are looking for you. If they find Uriel here, then they will find you. I cannot have that happen."

I held onto his hand, not wanting him to go but not able to voice that desire. Instead, I pushed up on my toes and pressed my mouth to his, not caring that Uriel was watching with utter disgust. Michael kissed me back like his life depended on it.

For all I knew it might have. It certainly felt like it to me.

When he released me, I felt warm all over and desperately didn't want him to leave.

"Gabriel will take my place in a few moments." Michael brushed his lips against mine once more before moving away. His eyes locked with Uriel's, and then, with a quick jerk of his head, he disappeared. Uriel thankfully went along with him.

Staring longingly at the spot he had been standing, I wondered if that was the last time that I would see him. Would he come back? Or would Uriel keep him away?

All the way in my car on my way back to my apartment, my mind whirled. It kept going down that path of no return, to the day that they would inevitably leave me. I wasn't naive. I knew what we were doing wasn't going to last, not in the long term. In many ways, Uriel was right. Not that I'd tell him that, but still it made my heart hurt.

As I pounded up the stairs of my apartment building, I had only one thing on my mind, drowning out the voice in my head with alcohol.

Without worry or precaution, I threw open my apartment door and headed straight for the cabinet where I knew I had a bottle of vodka hiding behind the olive oil.

"Someone isn't having a good day."

I glanced over my shoulder, my hand up in the cabinet to see Gabriel dressed in a tight, dark blue t-shirt and low hanging jeans leaning against the edge of the couch.

"Hey, want to be my drinking buddy?" I lifted the bottle from the cabinet and brought it to my chest. "I'm having a lousy day and could use someone to day drink with." I paused for a moment. "Can angels even get drunk?"

Gabriel arched a brow. "I wouldn't know. I've never drank."

"Well," I grinned and spun the lid of the bottle, "today is as good of day as any to find out!"

I pricked my finger and offered it to him. With an amused grin, Gabriel walked over and took my finger into his mouth. The sucking sensation pulled my mind away from getting drunk to doing other naughty things, but I didn't let it dissuade me. There was no reason I couldn't do both.

"Alcohol first." I took a long drink from the bottle and coughed as it burned on the way down.

"Your turn." I held the bottle out to Gabriel, and he took it gingerly, reading the words on the label before bringing it to his lips.

He took a long drink, much longer than I had, enough that I had to reach out and grab the bottle before he downed it all.

"Hey, now. Don't drink it all. You'll kill yourself. Or well, maybe not but still, you need to share." I furrowed my brows at him, already feeling the effects of the alcohol. "Maybe we should just use cups."

I moved back to the cabinet and grabbed two shot glasses. Pouring the vodka into the glasses, I shoved one toward Gabriel as I leaned against the counter.

"So, tell me, oh angelic one, what's it like in heaven?"

Gabriel took the glass and stared at it before tipping it back in one go. I watched his throat move up and down as he swallowed, mesmerized by his very presence. Man, that vodka was working fast. Had I eaten today? Nope. Nothing but that frozen yogurt with Michael. Oh, well. I wanted to get drunk. Guess I would be getting tacos later.

"Heaven is..." Gabriel trailed off, holding his tiny shot glass in his big hand as he stared off into the distance. "Energy. It's not like here where everything is hard and cold." His lips pressed together and then he ran his tongue across his teeth. I felt like a drooling idiot watching him. "We don't even look like this up there." He gestured to his form. "That's all for the sake of you humans."

"Huh." I leaned my face on my hand as my vision grew blurry. "Then how do you know who is who? Are you like Tinkerbelle? Sparkling little lights flying through the sky?" I made a zooming noise as my hand pretended to be a plane jetting through the clouds.

"Tinkerbelle?"

I dropped my arm and met his gaze. "You know, like a fairy?"

"Fairies aren't real," he said simply, but before he could even finish, I jumped up and clamped my hands over his mouth, my eyes wide.

"Don't say that!"

He tried to talk around my hands, but I wouldn't drop them.

"Every time you say that, a fairy somewhere falls down dead." I stared at him, dead serious. His brows shot up to his forehead, and I could feel him smiling against my hand. "You laugh but it's true.

Just ask Peter Pan." I dropped my hand and poured another shot for us both.

"Who?"

"Never mind." I waved him off and downed my shot. As that burned its way down my throat, I grabbed the bottle of vodka and walked away from the counter and toward my bed. In mid-stride, I kicked my shoes off, then sat the bottle down by the bed. Pulling my shirt off, I stood in my bra and pants. "Are you coming or what?"

Gabriel stared at me for a moment, and then realization kicked in and he hurried to my side.

Beaming up at him, I unbuttoned my pants and dropped them to the floor before kicking them away. "Okay, your turn."

Gabriel swallowed hard and then, like lightning, had all his clothes off and stood completely nude before me. I gaped at his body, all the lines and hard muscle, before I hurried to catch up with him. In my hurry, I ended up tangled in my own underwear and fell to the bed in a moan of mortification.

"Well, that was sexy," I grunted as I slapped a hand over my face, not chancing a look at the angel before me.

"Very." Gabriel chuckled and the bed dipped beside me. "I've never seen a more arousing sight."

His words were low and seductive, making me move my hand away from my face to see him hovering over me. His eyes weren't on my sprawled-out form but my pink face.

Flushing even harder, I waved him off. "Stop it. You're embarrassing me."

Gabriel only laughed louder before picking up on of my legs and trailing his mouth along my ankle. The sensation made me shiver and my embarrassment evaporated. I watched with a gaping mouth as his lips moved up my calf, my knee, and then slowed along the inside of my thigh. My heart rate sped up in anticipation of where he would go next, but instead of giving me what I so desperately desired, Gabriel skipped right over my center and went to the other ankle and started over from the beginning.

By the time he reached my core once more, I was begging for him to touch me. Taste me. Anything to ease the pulsating need inside of me.

"Gabriel," I panted as I reached for him. "Please."

"Oh, I do so love it when you beg." Gabriel's eyes lit up and his lips curled into a mischievous smile.

"I'll beg all night long if you would just fuck me

already," I growled at him, getting a hold of his arm and pulling him toward me. He didn't budge. With a narrowed gaze, I bared my teeth at him. "Come on, no more teasing."

"But I thought you liked it," Gabriel murmured as he lowered himself down to hover above my core. His words were hot against my skin, and a low moan escaped my throat. "You like to want it so badly, you might die before you get it."

His tongue flattened against me and I gasped, my hips bucking up to meet him.

"Gabe." I said his name like a prayer on my lips, and he must have liked it because he didn't make me beg for him to do it again. His mouth covered me, pulling and lapping at my most sensitive parts until I was falling apart at the seams.

Then, while I was still trying to catch my breath, my alcohol-muddled mind spinning, he climbed up to place his arms on either side of my shoulders. Our gazes locked together, blue eyes meeting green, as he slid home. My legs automatically wrapped around his waist, and he rocked against me.

Low keening sounds slipped out of my mouth while his pace quickened. My fingers dug into his biceps, urging him to go faster, harder. He didn't make me beg for it. Maybe he was tired of waiting too, or maybe he needed this as much as I did.

Gabriel moved inside of me at a breakneck speed, and he was still going even when I came and started to build up to another orgasm. It wasn't until I'd come again that Gabriel finally let out a grunt and slowed down, now just rocking against me to ride out the feeling.

My hands played with the hair on the back of his, neck and I smiled up at him. He returned my smile with one of his own and a soft kiss. Against my better judgement, or maybe because of the alcohol, I let those words I so wanted to say fly out of my mouth.

"I love you."

18

Gabriel stared down at me like I'd grown a second head. "You love me?"

I eyed him as I pulled my lower lip into my mouth. "Is that okay?"

Shifting off me, Gabriel sat on the edge of the bed his hand and ran a hand through his hair, mussing it more. "I mean, I guess. I don't know."

"What do you mean you don't know?" I sat up on the bed, my irritation starting to cover up my hurt. "Either it is, or it isn't. Either you feel something, or you don't."

I must have been putting off some kind of distress signal because Lucifer appeared at that very moment. Dressed in one of his usual suits that made my mouth water on most occasions, his dark eyes zeroed in on Gabriel and mine's state of undress and a wicked grin slid up his face.

"Well, well, looks like I missed out on some fun." His expression changed when he read our faces. "What is it? Did he not get you off? Don't feel bad, brother. It happens to the best of us." Lucifer adjusted the cuffs of his shirt beneath his jacket sleeves. "After all—"

"She said she loved me." Gabriel's eyes moved from the ground to Lucifer, his words stopping the Devil in the middle of his rambling. "Did she tell you?"

As if he saw something in Lucifer's eyes, Gabriel turned to me next and asked with a sort of panicked voice, "Do you love him too? What about Michael?"

"She told me too, mate." Lucifer's brow furrowed. "No need to get so worked up. It's only natural she'd fall for us. We are quite irresistible." He pulled at the sides of his jacket as he grinned and winked my way.

Frustrated beyond measure, I shifted on the bed to pull the covers up. Naked and real talk don't really go together. "So far, I'm just hearing a bunch of talk about me loving you, but none of you have yet to say you loved me. Feeling a bit loveless here!"

Gabriel didn't turn to me, but Lucifer made a sort of surprised sound.

"Love, we're angels," he said softly. "I'm not sure we even define love as the same thing."

"But you love God, don't you?" I pointed out, my confidence shrinking by the second. "That's the same thing."

"No, it's not." Gabriel's body twisted around to look at me. "We love God because he created us to be that way. We want what he wants. We need to make him happy. It's in our DNA."

"What about him?" I jerked a hand at Lucifer as my face scrunched together in confusion. "He clearly doesn't love God. He fell."

Lucifer scowled. "For the last time, I didn't fall. I disagreed with dear old dad, and he is punishing me for it. That doesn't mean I don't feel the same as the rest of them." He pointed a finger to his head, letting a wry grin slid up his face. "It's like a needle in your head telling you to do this or that, and you fight against it, but you can't stop it. So, one might argue that I disagreed because he wanted me to, and thus, I am being punished for no reason."

I would have felt sorry for the Devil right then had it not been for the fact that I had already bared my heart to them, and they were systematically stomping all over it.

"So, what do you feel for me?" I asked, trying a different tactic. I held the covers to my chest as my head whipped back and forth between the two of them, dying for an answer to my question.

Gabriel reached out and took my hand. His thumb brushed along the top of my knuckles. While the movement was soothing, it wasn't enough to make me give up on my question. Finally, he spoke.

"I care for you deeply. I want to be with you when I'm not here. I think about you all the time. I'd put myself between you and the rest of Heaven's army if it came down to it." He paused for a moment, his eyes full of emotion and insecurity. "Is that love? The kind you have?"

I swallowed down the tears that threatened to fall and nodded. "Oh, yes. Definitely."

Moving closer to me, Gabriel cupped my cheek and stroked the tears that I hadn't been able to catch.

"Then I love you, Jane Mehr."

I dropped the sheet and flung myself at him, holding him tightly to me. He laughed and hugged me back, then began to press kisses to my shoulders and neck. Before I could let him start something else, I lifted my head from his shoulder and met Lucifer's gaze.

Those dark eyes met mine and were filled with such mixed feelings that I almost thought he didn't feel the same way. Then I remembered the way he had needed me to say it. He needed me to love him because he didn't know if he was just a byproduct of his father's creation or if he was his own man.

I mouthed, *I love you*, to the Devil.

With that, he nodded and smiled back at me. He didn't need to say the words to get his point across. It took a long moment, but when we had all calmed down, I leaned back from Gabriel.

"Well, I guess that sobered me up enough that I should finish my work for the day," I muttered.

After I stood from the bed, I searched for my clothes, well aware of the hot gazes on my bare body. So I might have taken my time finding my clothes. So I might have wiggled my ass a bit more than usual. I was a girl in love with three hot angels, could you blame me?

"Jane," Lucifer groaned. "If you expect to leave this apartment, you need to hurry it up, love. As the master of torture, I can only stand so much of it."

Giving him an impish grin, I stopped teasing

and pulled my clothes back on. Gabriel followed suit and hid all that delectable flesh from my view.

"So, are you both coming to this person's house?" I cocked my head to the side and picked up my keys. "I only have one person left to ask about the trophy, and if this doesn't pan out, I might have to call it quits."

"Well, we wouldn't want that, now do we, pet?" Lucifer grinned, his hands in his pockets. "It'd ruin our reputation. Come, Gabriel, we will solve this mystery for our lady love, or we should turn in our wings now."

Gabriel nodded in agreement and followed me to the door. I stopped as I remembered something. Pulling out the pin, I started to prick myself, but Lucifer stopped me.

"Don't." My eyes jerked to him questioningly. "As much as I want to be physical, if I became whole right now, we'll never the leave apartment." The liquid lust in his eyes made my lower parts clench tight in need.

Reluctantly, I nodded and put the pin back in my shirt. "Come on, no rest for the wicked."

"Don't I know it," Lucifer rumbled after us, making us all laugh.

Once we were all in the car, I pulled out the

address to the last and final contestant that I needed to check up on, Chloe Wong. She lived in the better part of town, close to my parents in fact, which didn't lead me to believe she would want to talk to us. Well, maybe Gabriel, if she swung that way.

"So, what are we looking for, love?" Lucifer asked me as we pulled up to Chloe's overpriced condo. "Bloody knife? Falsified records? Lying about tax deductions?"

"How do you even know about any of that stuff?" I glanced over my shoulder at him.

Lucifer shrugged. "I'm the Devil. I hear a lot of stuff. You'd be surprised by all the wicked things I know." He wagged his eyebrows at me suggestively.

"Come on." I rolled my eyes as I exited the car and walked up to the condo's locked door. Great, I had to be let in to see her. That was going to go well. After finding the number on the board for Chloe's condo, I pushed in the call button for that number. It rang and rang and rang but there was no answer. With a frown, I glanced back to double-check number and pressed it again. Still no answer.

As I was contemplating calling the next number down, an older woman came out of the building. I moved aside to let her by while giving her an inno-cent smile. She nodded at me and then openly ogled Gabriel. As soon as she passed, I caught the closing door just as Gabriel made a surprised sound.

"What?" I asked as I hurried inside.

"That old lady just grabbed my butt." Gabriel gaped at where the old lady walked down to her car parked in the handicap spot. "I didn't think human libidos lasted that long."

I laughed, well, more like I cackled. "Oh, God. Yes, they do. You'd be surprised at how high the rate of STDs is in old folk's homes. They have nothing else to do but watch TV and boink like bunnies. Well, and wait to die, but still, what a way to go, huh?" I grinned at the two of them as they shook their heads in disbelief.

Really, I applauded the old gal. If I was an old lady, I'd be using all kinds of excuses to do what I wanted to but couldn't have done when I was younger. I was going to die anyway, so might as well go out with a bang.

We took the elevator up to the third floor without incident. As we moved down the hallways, I searched for Chloe's condo number. It only took a few moments to find it, so we approached it as if we were just normal visitors.

I knocked on the door. Nothing. I glanced back at the guys.

"What now?" I asked thoughtfully.

Gabriel looked at Lucifer and shrugged. "Why don't you go in and see if she's home?"

"I'm not a bloody ghost." Lucifer sighed as he walked towards the door. "I'm the Devil. I shouldn't—"

Whatever else he said was cut off as he disappeared into the door. We waited a few moments and then I called out to him.

"Lucifer?" I tried to yell-whisper so that the neighbors wouldn't get suspicious. "Did you find anything?"

Lucifer didn't answer for a minute, but finally, his head popped back through the door. "Well, she's not here, I can tell you that."

"Huh?" I angled my head to the side. "What do you mean?"

Coming completely out of the condo, Lucifer straightened his suit out. "The entire place has been emptied out. In a hurry too. Didn't even grab the food in the fridge."

"Well," I sighed as I placed a hand on my hip, "if that doesn't say guilty than I don't know what does." I pulled my phone out, wondering if Andre had a forwarding address for our Ms. Chloe Wong.

"Hold on." Gabriel placed a hand on my shoulder. "I'm getting a vision." His eyes clouded over, and he had a far off look on his face. A tight frown formed on his lips as he tried to concentrate on what he was seeing. "There's a woman in a tight dress with dark hair."

"Chloe Wong?" I asked as I glanced over at Lucifer. "Did you see a picture of her? What does she look like?"

Lucifer stroked his chin. "Well, the whole apartment was empty, so I'd say that's a no."

I sighed, pulling my phone out. I typed in 'Chloe Wong designer' into the search bar. A picture of a thirty something year old woman of Asian descent appeared on the screen. I flipped to her social media pages and panned through her pictures and then held it out to Gabriel.

"Is this her?"

Gabriel's eyes cleared over and his face relaxed. As he turned toward me, he took the phone. "Yes, this is the woman I saw. She was talking to a large man in a suit near a warehouse off the interstate."

I took my phone back and flipped to the section of pictures displaying her designs. Immediately, I grimaced. "Ugh. If anyone needs help to win this contest, it would be her."

"Oh, dear lord." Lucifer made a disgusted sound as he looked over my shoulder. "Are those pastels and plaid? Together?"

I giggled. "Yep."

"Even I wouldn't subject my torture victims to that kind of madness and I'm the Devil." He buttoned his suit jack and shook his head.

"So, the vision." I turned to Gabriel, arching a brow. "What did you see? Exactly."

Gabriel ran a hand through his hair as he shook his head. "Not much more than that honestly. There were a lot of cars and vans parked around, but it pretty much looked like they were hanging out."

"Okay," I said, dragging the word out. "Do you have any idea what warehouse or what interstate?" I couldn't imagine there were many, but the more details, the better.

Gabriel's eyes squinted as he tried to see more. "Interstate eighty-seven, the building says Dress Factory Wholesale." His vision became clear again. "Does that help?"

"Yeah." I nodded as I headed for the door. "Now, to catch them in the act before they flee."

19

On the drive to the warehouse from Gabriel's vision, a call came through. Since I was driving, I had Gabriel answer it.

"Hello, Jane's phone," he managed at last. "Who is this?"

I could barely contain my laughter at the sight of the big gorgeous angel holding the phone a few inches from his ear like it might bite him at any moment. They really did need to get with the times already. I was only one woman. I could only do so much.

On the phone Mandy's voice came through from the other side, quite irate. "Mandy. Put Jane on the phone."

Gabriel gave me a sideways look. "Jane's driving."

The annoyed growl pouring out of my phone made Gabriel lean away from it, a painted look on his face.

With a roll of my eyes, I slowed down so I could gesture to him without crashing. "Put it on speaker phone."

Gabriel looked at the device, his brows furrowed. "How?"

"Just push the screen so it wakes up." I held a finger up to show him what to do. "Now, push that symbol that looks like a speaker. No." I shook my head. "That's mute. The other one."

"Jane. Jane? Are you there?" Mandy's voice came out louder than before, and Gabriel sat back with a pleased expression.

"Such a clever device," Lucifer commented, leaning between the seats to look over the phone. "Much easier than trying to tap into the right mind."

I glanced over at him. "You read each other's minds?"

"Only when we're on the divine plane of existence."

"Jane, are you talking to one of the others?"

Mandy asked, exasperated by being left out of the conversation. "Look, whatever, I have news I thought you might want to know."

"Sorry, yeah. Lucifer is here but not physical." I smirked as I put my eyes back on the road. "Gabriel was the one who answered the phone. I'm heading toward a warehouse where Gabriel said the last contestant is at and talking to some shady looking guy."

"You mean Sirgio Cortez?" Mandy asked curiously.

I frowned. "I'm going to pretend I know who that is."

"Well, that's the name registered to that number we got from Noah," she explained. "Sirgio Cortez, he's a minor criminal with mob connections. They have their hands in a lot of things. Gas, medical, even the fashion industry. It's not surprising they would want to rig the contest."

"What's this Sirquini guy look like?" I asked as I pushed down on the accelerator.

"Sirgio," Mandy corrected me with a huff. "Judging from his mug shot and his file, he's five foot five with a goatee. Brown hair and eyes. Caucasian. Three cheeseburgers short of a heart attack."

"Sound like our guy?" I shot a look over at Gabriel.

"Besides the cheeseburger thing, yes. It does sound like the man I saw with Chloe, but he certainly wasn't eating cheeseburgers," Gabriel explained before exchanging a look with Lucifer.

I could just imagine what they were thinking. Humans and their weird references. Well, I had something to say about them and the celestial garbage they spewed sometimes. It was like deciphering hieroglyphs.

"Well, okay," I said as I continued ignoring them. "We have a designer who got paid to drop out, someone who wanted to buy the judges names from Noah, and a missing trophy. I bet you a hundred bucks they're all from this Sergargo guy."

"You're making it worse," Mandy scoffed. "But, yeah, it does look that way. You said someone named Chloe was with them? I requested Sirgio's bank records to see if anything shady was there to link him to the case. He was already on our watch list for mob activity, so it wasn't hard to get a judge to help me out."

"Okay, and that means?" I tapped the steering wheel, waiting for her to get to the point.

"He send a money transfer to a Chloe Wong last Friday. Right before—"

"The trophy went missing," I finished for her with a smile and a nod. "We've got our bad guys."

"We've got our bad guys," Mandy repeated and then asked, "What's your heading? I'll meet you out there with backup."

"You think we'll need it?" I frowned. The last people I had to get involved in this, the better.

"Well, you never know when guys like these might bring guns. Do you have a gun?" Mandy's voice sounded like she half-expected me to even though I wasn't supposed to have one.

"Uh, no, but I do have two bad ass angels," I quipped. "Does that count?"

"To the law?" Mandy paused. "No. So, I expect you to keep them in line when we go confront this guy."

"Fine," I huffed. I glanced over at Gabriel and Lucifer. "You heard her, boys, you're to be on your best behavior."

Lucifer snorted. "Well, I'm incorporeal so not a problem here."

"Hey, I'm only here for Jane." Gabriel lifted his hand, the one not holding the phone. "I'll do as she asks."

I rolled my eyes, because no way was that statement true. He rarely did what I wanted.

"Alright," I said towards the phone, "we're heading north on I-87. Toward the Dress Factory. You know where that is?"

"Yeah," Mandy responded, it sounded like she was typing on the other side. "I can find it. I'll meet you there."

"Okay, over and out."

I started to ask Gabriel to hang up, but Mandy added, "And Jane? Wait for me."

"Ugh. Fine. I will wait like a good little psychic detective until the big bad police show up." I scrunched my nose up and reached out, turning off the phone before she could continue.

"Are you two always like that?" Lucifer asked, grinning at me.

"You've been around me this long, and you're still asking about my relationships with people?" I turned us off the interstate towards the warehouse Chloe and Spaghetti-O was supposed to be meeting at. "Mandy and I have been best friends most of our lives. If I had anyone I could count on, it's her." Gabriel made a sound of alarm. "Okay, you two too, but Mandy doesn't have to suck my blood like some freaking vampire to touch me." I smiled suddenly. "Then again, I would never do the kind of touching I do to you with Mandy."

"Pity." Lucifer winked.

I snorted as I turned off into a parking lot a bit away from where Gabriel directed. Best to maintain every element of surprise we could. Once we were parked, I unbuckled my seatbelt and turned to my angels.

"Look," I explained frankly. "This might get hairy, so just do what Mandy says and let me run the show."

Before either of them could complain, I climbed out of the car and headed toward the warehouse proper. Around the back, I could see vans parked around a loading dock where several people were hanging around and talking.

Keeping close to the side of the building for cover, I snuck up past the dock and behind one of the vans to peer around the corner and get a closer look. Five people. One of them was a short female that had to be Chloe, and another matched Mandy's description of the big guy from the mob.

"Is this what you call waiting for backup?" Gabriel asked as he snuck up behind me. He leaned against the side of the van, not even bothering to hide while I crouched down low. Lucifer wasn't even hiding behind the vehicle, just standing there in plain daylight and grinning like a fiend.

"I call this finding out what we're dealing with before the backup shows up and steals all the thunder I worked hard to get paid for," I whispered back at him. Then, I crept closer, inching my way forward until I was just at the front bumper. I peeked around the fender and came face to face with a pair of boots. I followed those boots up a pair of legs and then a gun pointed at my face. Giving the creepy guy holding the gun a meek smile, I waved.

"Uh, hi. I heard I can get some great discounts here."

"Get up." The goon pushed the gun closer to me, and I followed it up off the ground and put my hands in the air.

Gabriel shifted behind me, tensed to spring into action, but I held out towards him. I didn't want him to hurt anyone if we didn't have to, even though they were being threatening first.

"Out from behind the van." The man gestured toward where the others were waiting. Another man no less welcoming appeared around the other side to lead Gabriel and me out to the group of people. Chloe was in the center of them.

"Who's this?" Sirgio pulled the cigar he'd been smoking out of his mouth and gestured toward me with mild interest. When he saw Gabriel, any amusement in his face disappeared. Jerking his eyes to Chloe, he grunted, "These friends of yours?"

"No," Chloe Wong answered. The woman had a severe frown on her face that made her look all the more ball-busting than the tight red dress and long earrings she wore. She looked like a man eater about to chow down on her dinner. "I've never seen them before in my life."

"Are you sure?" Sirgio looked us over and chuckled. "This one here looks like he could be one of those models you use. And this one, well, if she isn't a model…" I touched my hair, smiling slightly at the compliment I figured was coming. "… then she's someone's assistant."

Fuck you too, buddy.

"No, never." She narrowed her laser glare on us, no doubt wondering herself where we came from.

"Why don't I introduce myself?" I lowered my hands and placed one on my chest. "I'm Jane. This is Gabriel. We're just checking out the warehouse. I was told I could find some discounted brand names here. Was that wrong?" I glanced around at the thugs circling us, trying to look meek and innocent.

"This warehouse hasn't been operational in years." Sirgio chuckled and waved his cigar at me. "Try again, doll."

"I told you, my friend told me I could get—"

Sirgio nodded to the thug on the right next to Gabriel. He cocked his gun and pointed it at Gabriel's head. "What was that?"

"Okay," I gasped as I held my hands back up. "Okay, okay. I'm not looking for a sale. I'm a psychic detective, and I'm on a case."

"Psychic detective?" Chloe laughed haughtily. "People actually believe in that stuff?"

"Actually, you'd be surprised." I arched a brow at her. "Anyway, I'm trying to find a trophy. I don't care about the rest of whatever is going on here." I waved a hand around the group. "My job description says to find a golden trophy that's it. The rest is all you." I pointed at Chloe and Sirgio. "You want to take over the fashion world, be my guest, I won't judge." I shrugged.

Sergeant Spaghetti laughed, a big belly laugh that made his stomach and chin fat shake. He gestured to one of his guys, and they brought a brief case over. With a moment's fiddling, he popping the top open to reveal the very trophy I had been hired to find.

"I like you," he said as he arched a hairy eyebrow at me. "You're funny. As you can see, we have the trophy, but why would we give it to you?"

I grinned, blinking my lashes at him. "Out of the goodness of your heart?"

"Ha. Ha. Ha. Ha." He shook his head and kept laughing so much so I thought he might have a heart attack. He breathed heavily and then put the cigar in the side of his mouth. "How about this? I'll only kill lover boy here, and then you're free to go with a vow of silence... or we will come silence you."

I glanced to Gabriel and then back to the big guy. Shaking my head, I sighed. "Sorry, I'm kind of attached to him. Besides, God might get a bit pissed off at me if I got his messenger killed."

That very real but very strange statement confused the goons just long enough for me to jerk forward and grab the trophy. I spun around and ran before they realized what a stupid move I had pulled.

"That was your big plan?" Lucifer called out after me as I ran.

See, I figured Gabriel could keep up or go incorporeal if he really needed to. Me, I wasn't so lucky, so I bobbed and weaved in a zig-zag motion toward the car. I mean, that's what they did on all those cop shows to avoid getting shot, right?

Good thing I did, as bullets whizzed by my head and hit the ground just as I shifted to the right.

"So?" I shrugged, getting out of breath. "I improvised."

"What are you doing?" Gabriel jogged up next to me. "I can carry you if you keep running around like that."

Shooting him a glare, I dove behind the nearest van. The sound of bullets sprayed the side, making me flinch with every sound. "I'm doing evasive running. It makes me a harder target. How'd you get through it?"

"I'm faster than them." Gabriel laughed. "And it makes you look like you're having an episode."

I huffed and glowered. "Well, then next time you can grab the goods, and I'll be the all-powerful being waltzing through the bullet spray," I huffed as I glowered at him.

"Come on, we have to keep moving." Before I could start doing exactly that or even get a word out edgewise, Gabriel grabbed me by the waist and tossed me over his shoulder like a sack of potatoes.

Tensing up, I covered my head with the trophy and peeked out at the guys running after us. They had made it to the van now and they were quickly closing in on us.

"We're not going to make it. Where's that angel speed at?" I yelled at him, smacking him on the ass. "Get a move on!"

Gabriel huffed a laugh. "Alright, hold on tight."

I bounced up and down as he increased his speed and I forgot about dodging bullets and more about keeping from knocking myself out. Wrapping my arms around his waist, I held on tight as my body felt like it was being squished against a wall.

Just as we hit the parking lot where I parked, sirens sounded as Mandy's car screeched into the lot, skidding to a halt right in front of us.

"Yay, the cavalry has arrived!" I threw my hands in the air from my awkward position over Gabriel's shoulder as Mandy and O'Connor climbed out of their vehicle. Two squad cars pulled up next to them and disgorged another four cops, guns drawn and ready for anything.

"What part of wait for me didn't you understand?" Mandy yelled at me as she took in the sight of me holding the trophy triumphantly and the pack of gun-toting goons running our way.

Gabriel sat me on my feet, and I shrugged. "Did you really think I was going to listen?"

Shaking her head, she gestured for her fellow officers to follow her lead as she pulled her badge out and high for the mobsters to see.

"BFPD!" she shouted with every bit of cop authority she could muster, and trust me, with Mandy, that was a lot. "Put your weapons down!"

The goons slowed down but didn't drop their pistols. One of them leaned their head to the side as they were listening into an ear piece, and then, one by one, they sat their guns on the ground.

I gave Gabriel the trophy and followed after Mandy. Before I could get two steps, O'Connor stepped between me and the rest of the action.

"No, you don't. You've caused enough problems for today, don't you think?" His green eyes sparkled with satisfaction at the very thought of me in trouble. "You're lucky you have Stevenson to help you out or you'd be Swiss cheese right now. You should really rethink this whole profession, if you can't even shoot a gun."

I resisted the urge to flip him off as I backed away to sit with Gabriel by our car. Staring hard at where Mandy and the cops disappeared behind the vans, I contemplated jumping in the car and booking it.

I inched toward the driver seat and then I saw a

streak of red dart, the color of Chloe's dress as she ran across the parking lot and followed by the big man, Sergio. I ran to my driver side door, jerked it open, and cranked the engine to speed toward them.

Lucifer appeared in the backseat, a bemused expression on his face. "Where are you going, love?"

I grinned back at him as I angled the car toward the fleeing crooks and then whipped my steering wheel to the left as I slammed on the brakes. With the sound of skidding tires on asphalt, I pulled the car around into a spin and landed it right in the path of Chloe Wong and Sergio. They didn't have time to stop and ran right into my car. Well, Chloe did. Sergio, I think, passed out from exhaustion. I rolled down my window just as Mandy and the others came up behind them.

"Maybe next time you give you'll think twice before not taking my offer," I shouted down at the two perps as the cops swooped in to make their arrests.

20

Mandy and the other cops got Chloe and Sergio locked down with their goons. The entire time they were being cuffed, the little designer spat curses and swore to call her lawyer on all of us. There was a lot of moaning, bitching, and general disgruntlement among the goons before they all got tucked off into patrol cars and carted off to jail. Naturally, because of my integral part in saving the day, I had to come along with Mandy to make a statement, give evidence, all that sort of important police stuff.

"So, what did they want the trophy for?" I asked Mandy once we were done with all the boring stuff. I held the trophy up and flopped it down on my other hand.

"Well, it looks like Sergio wanted to steal the trophy so he could start his own competition," Mandy explained. "He and his friends in the mob were looking to get their foot in the door of the fashion scene. Something to do with money laundering, guns, drugs, the whole shebang." Mandy waved her hand in the air.

I frowned as I swung my feet in the chair by her desk. "Why didn't he just get his own trophy? Why steal Andre's?"

Mandy lifted a shoulder and dropped it as she began filling out paperwork. "I don't know, poetic justice?" She paused and sat the pen down. "By the way, while we're talking about it, we're going to need that trophy."

"But it's Andre's!" I pouted and clutched it to my chest as if it were my precious. "I need to give it back to him so I can get paid."

"You'll get it back." Mandy held her hand out, wiggling her fingers at me. "I promise. We have to log it with the rest of the evidence until the case is closed. Then, when it's done, Andre can come and claim his property."

"But how will he know that I found it and not you?" My eyes narrowed on her as I still held the trophy close.

Mandy arched a brow. "Do you really trust me so little?" I didn't answer her. "Man, decades together and still, you question my loyalty? You will get credit, don't worry."

"On your honor of our friendship." I held my pinkie out to her with a firm look.

"No."

"Then swear on orgasmic garlic bread."

Rolling her eyes, Mandy looped her pinkie with mine. "There, I promise. Now give it."

With a reluctant frown, I sat the trophy on the table and crossed my arms, turning my head away from it. "I always wanted a trophy, you know. I never win anything."

"That's because you always quit half way," Mandy pointed out as she took the trophy and put it into an evidence bag.

I sat up straighter and glared. "I do not quit everything."

"Oh, really?" Mandy laughed. "There was the ballet."

"The shoes hurt."

"Gymnastics."

"Nobody is that bendy." I shook my head, wincing at the thought of the fateful back bend that had ended my short career.

"What about the flute?" Mandy pointed out. "You were actually good at that, and you quit after one semester."

"Too much practice." I shrugged. "I had to think of my social life. Really, it was a charity for me to quit, that way Rachel Wick could take first chair. She needed something to be happy for with her grandmother being such a witch."

With a slow shake of her head, Mandy turned back to her paperwork. "If you say so, but still, I'm just waiting for the moment you quit this too."

"I will not. I'm made for this." I pointed at the trophy. "I have yet to lose a case."

"That's true." Mandy gave me a smile.

"What about Chloe?" I asked and leaned forward to tap my nails on the desk top. "Why was she in all this? Did she say?"

Mandy pushed away the paperwork, seeming to give up since I wasn't going to stop bugging her any time soon. "She said that she was tired of those fake posers winning all the time. It was time for someone with real talent to win for a change." Tightening her pony tail, Mandy made a bored face. "Seems like pretty normal stuff to me."

"Uh, no." I huffed. "Have you seen her stuff? She wasn't winning for a very specific reason and that's because her stuff sucked. Not because she wasn't like the rest of them."

"No, I haven't." Mandy turned her eyes to her computer, not interested in seeing what Chloe designed. Regardless of if she cared or not, I pulled out my phone and showed her. Squinting her eyes, Mandy stared at the phone. "Is that plaid? With pastels?"

"Yep." I nodded firmly. "She needs to die a horribly tragic death to make up for even bringing this crap into the world."

Mandy gave me a look. "You're in a police station. Could you please refrain from talking about killing people so freely? I'd hate to have to bail you out again."

"Hey!" I held a finger up and pointed it at her. "That was one time, and that ass wipe had it coming."

"If you say so." Mandy stood from her desk and picked up the trophy before walking toward the evidence room.

I jumped up and followed after her. Gabriel and Lucifer had taken off shortly after the police had gotten the bad guys down and hadn't come back yet. I figured they had something else to do besides watch me get paid. I hadn't seen those other two angels again either, Raphael and Azrael. Not that I wanted to see them, but the longer they stayed gone, the better. Nothing good would come of either of them appearing.

"I do say so." I stopped by Mandy as she filled out the forms to hand over my meal ticket. I watched it with sad reluctance. "He tried to cop a feel."

"And that required you breaking his hand with a metal door?" Mandy didn't even glance up from the evidence form she had gotten from the room's clerk, but the disbelief in her voice spoke volumes.

"Better than what I had planned," I muttered as I crossed my arms over my chest with a pout. "I had planned on finding the wire cutters from the shop class and taking a few inches off... from between his legs."

"Ew. Stop." Mandy's nose scrunched up at the visual. "Please, can we not talk about penises and such at my work?"

The lady clerk behind the evidence counter gave Mandy and me an amused look. I smiled prettily at her and then turned to Mandy.

"You're the one using the p word. I was being a lady."

"Pfft. Sure, you were." Mandy handed the paper

back to the lady and moved away from the counter. "Now, I have real work to do, a load of papers to fill out, and I don't have time for you to talk my ear off."

"Fine. I understand when I'm not wanted." I sighed as I continued to trail after her.

"Do you?" Mandy stopped in the entry way to the main offices. "Because you haven't caught the hint yet."

I grinned and clasped my hands together in front of me, giving her my best 'I love you' eyes. "That's because I know you don't mean it."

"Believe me." She grabbed my shoulders and turned me toward the front door. "I mean it, now scoot. Don't you have a paycheck to collect?"

"Alright, alright," I called over my shoulder, waving goodbye. "I'll see myself out."

As I walked out of the police station, I whistled to myself. I'd caught the bad guy, I was about to get paid. I think that means I earned myself a big fat margarita. Nothing could possibly go wrong.

And, of course, that was where I fucked up.

The moment I stepped out of the police station, I came face to face with my newest stalkers, the aforementioned Raphael and Azrael.

"I don't have time for you guys right now," I said with a put-upon sigh.

"I am on a mission, a mission to get paid. Not to be mistaken for getting laid because that is a whole other thing all together. Not that it isn't just as gratifying." I hummed. "Okay, maybe more. You know, it's sex." I looked at their puzzled expressions. "So, you don't know but whatever. I gotta go."

"Are you sure you are sane?" Azrael asked, not getting the hint. He and Raphael moved to either side of me so that I was sandwiched between them. In most cases, that would have been a promising position, but with two unknown angels, it was just creepy.

"Yes, well, my mom had me tested once." I pulled my keys out of my pocket as I increased my pace. I hoped I could get to my car before they caused a scene, and by scene, I mean before they made me look like a crazy person yelling at rude ass angels.

"We'll get out of your hair if you make us physical." Raphael moved in front of me to block my path to the car. Well, not really, I could walk through him, but it was annoying.

"No," I simply said as I paused before my car. I

tapped my foot impatiently and waited for them to make their case and get out of my face.

"If you do not agree to help us, then we will have to change our tactics," Azrael said from me behind me. He was so close that I could feel the buzzing of his energy pressing against my back.

"Ooo, what are you going to do?" I waved my hands and made a face. "Annoy me to death?" Sucking it up, I shoved my hand through Raphael and unlocked my car. Jumping inside the car, I slammed it shut and hoped they wouldn't figure out how to get in it.

Azrael glared at me as I turned my car on and got ready to pull out of my parking spot. He moved to the hood of my car and held out his arms, his hands hovering over the top of it. I stared at him as if daring him to do something. After all, I didn't think any of them could be as scary or as powerful as Michael could be.

However, when the electrical system in my car started to sputter and then the car promptly shut off, I was proven wrong. I gritted my teeth and tried to crank the car once again. Nothing. It didn't even click. With that, I growled as I shoved my car door open and stalked over to the hood.

Continuing to ignore the two douchebag angels,

I popped open the hood and stared down at the engine in the vain hope I could figure out what the asshole had done to it. Of course, I didn't know crap about cars, so me looking at it was about as useful as a clown running a kitchen.

"What'd you do?" I snapped and slammed my hood back down. "Fix it."

Azrael crossed his arms over his chest, a smug expression on his face. "No."

"Fix it now or I'll..."

"Or you'll what?" Raphael came over to stand beside Azrael, his hands in his pockets and his expression no less smug than his partner. "Call your masters to help you?"

"First of all," I held a finger up, "nobody is my master. I'm my own freaking boss. Second of all, you bet your asses I'm going to call for them, then we'll see who is demanding who. Michael!" I called into the sky, hoping it would work because I had never really had to call them before. They always just showed up when I needed them.

"Go ahead." Azrael waved a hand at me with a grin. "Yell all you want. They won't come."

My brows furrowed, I didn't let him stop me. "Lucifer! Michael! Gabriel! One of you better get your butts down here and take care of these jerk-wads before I cut you off forever." I paused and realized what I'd just said. "Okay, maybe not forever, but for a very long time. You hear me!"

The two of them laughed harder the more I yelled at the sky, and it wasn't until Mandy came running out of the police station that I finally stopped.

"What the hell are you doing?" Mandy looked around us before stopping before me. "Someone called into the office that someone was screaming at nothing like a crazy person in the middle of the parking lot. Obviously, I figured it was you." She gestured at me with a sigh. "What's wrong? I thought you left."

"I was trying to, but things have gotten complicated." I glared at the nearby angels.

Mandy glanced around her hands on her hips. "I figured with all the yelling. Why were you yelling for them? Aren't they here?"

I hesitated to tell her and then figured I might as well. "Not exactly. It seems word has gotten around, and now the groupies won't leave me alone."

"Groupies?" Raphael scoffed. "You wish. We simply want what you offered the others so freely."

"Not gonna happen. I don't know you, and I wouldn't give you anything just on principle of you being an asshat." I slashed my arm through the air in finality.

Mandy glanced worriedly between me and where I glared at. "So, why don't you just leave? They can't hurt you, right?"

Eyes still on the angels, I answered, "Not technically, I guess, but they can make my life a living hell. Ergo my car won't start now."

Mandy's frown deepened. "Let me look."

She opened the hood and glanced around, then she pulled out the oil thingy and putted it back before closing the hood. "I have no idea. Just call a ride."

"We'll just stop that vehicle too." Azrael said with a cruel grin.

"Yeah, I got that," I snapped at him and then said to Mandy, "They'll just mess up that one too. So, for the moment, I'm stranded."

"And what about the others? Why aren't they answering?" Mandy turned her cop gaze on the angels though she couldn't see them. They could see her though, and I wondered if it would work on them.

"Ask them." I shook my head and gestured to where they stood. "These jerks are all confident my guys won't come, and based on my yelling the last ten minutes, I'm worried something has happened." Turning my eyes from Mandy to them, I poured all my vengeance into my words. "If anything has happened to them, if you hurt them or even harmed one hair on their gorgeous heads, then I will make sure you never become solid. Never. You got me?"

"Then we won't leave you alone until you do. We are not as busy as the others." Raphael smirked and moved closer to me as if to run his fingers along my arm. I smacked at him, scowling when my hand went through the air. "We have time. You'll give in eventually… or go mad."

Stepping so close that our noses would have touched, I snarled, "I'd rather die."

"Now, that won't be necessary." Michael's voice boomed through the parking lot which made the two Angels before me cringe.

I spun on my heels, crossed my arms over my chest, and scowled. "Where were you? Didn't you hear me calling?"

"Darling, the dead heard you calling for us." Lucifer appeared beside me, and that made Raphael jump even further back from me.

"Agreed." Gabriel appeared, wiggling a finger in his ear. "Not so loud next time. If I were solid

when you did that, you'd have broken my
ear drums."

"Then maybe, next time, you should come
when I call the first time and not an hour later." I
huffed and glared daggers at the three of them.
"Where were you?"

"We were otherwise detained." Michael crossed
his arms over his impressive chest and returned my
glare with an ice stare. However, the true target of
that stare wasn't me but the angels behind me.

"Michael, you have to understand we just want
the chance you three had." Azrael walked through
the car to stand between Michael and me. "You are
being selfish keeping the human to yourself."

"The fact that you don't even call her by her
name proves we shouldn't share her." Lucifer
unbuttoned his suit jacket and tucked his hands into
his pockets. "You wouldn't appreciate her."

Mandy's eyes jerked back and forth trying to
figure out what's going on. "What are they saying?
Do I need to shoot someone?"

"No, not yet." I laughed and waved her off.
"The guys showed up, and now, my stalkers are
getting an ass handing."

Gabriel snickered as he took the few steps over
to me. "Are you alright?"

"I'm fine," I angled my head back to look up at him, "but my car has seen better days. They did something to it." I shot Azrael an accusing look.

"Fix it." Michael's words to the two douche nozzles were hard and unyielding. They promised pain and lots of it if they refused.

"But Michael—" Azrael started but stuttered to a stop as Michael's blue eyes began to glow like lightning. That's a new trick I hadn't seen before. "As you wish, my liege." Azrael placed a fist to his chest and bowed slightly.

All of a sudden, my car came roaring back to life which caused Mandy and me to jump in place. Happy my car was alright, I hurried over to it and hugged its hood.

"Is my baby okay? Did that bad angel hurt you?"

"Ugh, don't talk to your car like it's alive, Jane," Mandy told me as she shook her head. "At least, try to pretend you're normal at my place of work."

"Sorry." I shrugged. "You knew I wasn't normal when you became friends with me, a little late to be complaining about it now."

Lucifer snorted. "Got that right, love."

"Are you good here?" Mandy asked, shooting a look around. "I've got work to do, and if you're not going to blow the place up, I need to get back."

I looked to Michael. "Are we okay?"

Michael ripped his eyes away from Azrael to meet mine. "Yes, we will take care of them. Go home, Jane. Gabriel, escort her."

Gabriel inclined his head and climbed into the car with me. Mandy headed back inside after I told her it was safe leaving only the four angels in the parking lot.

I watched Lucifer and Michael surround Azrael and Raphael as we backed out of the parking lot. "Are they going to be okay?"

"Yes," Gabriel murmured, his eyes unfocused and glazed over. "Everything will be fine."

For some reason, the way he said it made me not entirely believe him.

21

Gabriel hung out with me for a few days with no sign of the other two. I was finally able to get Andre his trophy back. He'd been so happy to get it back that he invited me *and* my boyfriends to a party on his yacht.

Which was where I was now. Off the coast of Blessed Falls with a couple dozen or so of Andre's friends and miles of water between us and land.

"This is great," I told Andre with a smile. "If this is what you do in your free time, then I think I would love to be rich."

Andre laughed and handed me a flute of champagne. "It does grow on you." He wore a completely white suit with a black t-shirt beneath.

Andre was the very definition of cool among the fashionable people on his yacht. For the first few minutes, I'd felt very out of place in my yellow sun dress, but soon, I was three glasses into the alcohol and didn't give a flip what any of them thought of me.

"So, I haven't seen any of your boyfriends today. Did you break up? Get tired of juggling so many?" Andre not so subtly had been trying to hit on me the entire time. He started with a hand on my lower back as he took me on a tour of his boat and introduced me to all the fancy people he knew. It seemed like the billionaire was pulling out all the stops to impress me, and I felt guilty.

I should be thrilled while I was living it up, but all I could think about was the short note Gabriel left me this morning before I headed out.

Something came up.

That was it. Nothing else. No 'I'll see you later.' or 'I love you.' Just 'something came up.' Like I was a casual girl he'd been seeing on the side. All this lack of attention was starting to give me a complex which in turn made it so I couldn't enjoy the fabulous party happening around me, or the attention of the attractive man trying his damnedest to get me to notice him.

"Uh, no." I tucked a dark lock behind my ear and avoided his gaze. "They're working. I'm sure they'll show up eventually."

"Well, we're not making dock for the rest of the day so they might have to set this one out." Andre picked up my hand and rubbed the top of my knuckles. "Which means... I get you all to myself."

I let out a nervous chuckle. "Yeah, seems like."

For more than once since I'd gotten there, I wish I hadn't come, at least not without one of the guys at my side. With them there, at least Andre was a bit less touchy feely with me. I didn't hate it or anything, but once you've been with an angel, it was kind of hard to enjoy spending time with regular old humans, and it showed.

"Would you like something to eat?" He steered me toward the buffet table they had set up in the middle of the first floor. The boat was idling off the coast, and the wind was just low enough to be nice and not hair destroying. Overall, it would be a perfect day for a party... if three people weren't missing.

"No, thank you." I waved a hand at the table. "I'm not hungry."

Andre let out a startled laugh. "You? Not hungry? Are you feeling alright?" I stared at him curiously. "I don't mean to laugh, but you took me as the kind of woman who was always eating. Or thinking about eating. I thought for sure I would have a win just for having food readily available."

I gave him a weak smile. "No, you had me pegged right. Food is my second love."

"And your first?"

Opening my mouth to answer him, I changed my mind and clamped it shut. I moved toward the table as I have him a polite nod. "I think I could probably eat just a little."

"Good." Andre ushered me over to the table with a chuckle. "I would hate to have left overs."

Normally, the fact that he liked a woman who could eat and actually encouraged it would have been a big plus in his column, but my mind was elsewhere. I only ate because I had nothing else to do, and it would keep him from making me talk too much to him. I know, right? Me not wanting to talk? It's a miracle. Or a curse. My stomach was swirling with worry, so it sure felt like it.

"So, are you working on any new cases yet?" Andre asked once we had our plates and were sitting at a small table off to the side of the dance floor. Several people came by to tell him what a great party he was throwing before I could get a word out.

"No, not right now." I shook my head and then shoved a meat ball in my mouth. I gave myself ample time to chew it and then chewed it even more for good measure before swallowing it down with more alcohol. At this point, my head was getting a bit fuzzy. I should probably slow down and switch to water. Our knees bumped against each other every so often from the cramped space which I think he did on purpose. I tried to keep myself turned away as much as possible.

"Probably taking a break to recharge your powers, huh?" Andre grinned at me, only picking at the food on his plate. I had a feeling that this party was just a ruse to get me to spend time with him since I'd turned down his offer for a date several times already.

I let out a long sigh. "Yeah, something like that."

He started to ask me something else, but something caught my eye. My gaze drew to the side where Uriel stood at the stern of the boat. His eyes were locked on me, and it was not a pleasant expression on his face. It made the food in my stomach turn sour.

"Jane?" Andre placed a hand on mine. "Are you alright?"

I jerked my eyes away from the angel. "Uh, no. Actually, I think I just feel a bit sea sick. I'm going to go to the bathroom." I stood from the table and moved toward the stairs leading into the lower level.

Once I got below deck, I searched for Uriel in the hope that he had taken the hint and had followed me down below. There weren't as many people down here as upstairs. Most of them wanted to take advantage of the nice day and sea breeze. Those who were down here weren't paying me any mind as they cuddled in corners or laughed as they tried to find an empty room to get it on in.

I found Uriel at the end of the long hallway, waiting impatiently for me to appear next to him.

"Where are they?" I asked right off the bat, not letting him steer the conversation.

"You have caused quite a stir. I do not think you are in a position to be demanding anything." Uriel's gaze bored into me, his voice crisp and to the point.

"I don't care what position you think I'm in. Gabriel left all of a sudden this morning, and I haven't seen the others in days. What's going on?" I wished he was corporeal so I could shove my finger into his chest to emphasis my point, but instead, I settled for banging my hand against the wall next to us. A couple of people glanced my way, but I ignored them. I wasn't in the mood to care about looking crazy today.

"They are doing what they should be doing. Their jobs." Uriel crossed his arms and stared me down. Well, if he thought I was just going to roll over and give in, then he had another thing coming. I was the champion of staring contests.

"That's never stopped them from coming before," I countered. "They've always come when I needed them. I need them now."

"It doesn't work that way anymore," Uriel snapped as he lost his patience. "They are no longer yours to command. You would do well to forget them and get on with your puny life while you still have one."

"Are you threatening me?" I stepped closer, angling my head back to see him clearly. It was hard to be intimidating when the guy had a good foot on you.

"Even if I was, there would be nothing you could do, human."

"Oh, yeah," I argued, nodding like a weirdo. "Oh, yeah." Okay, so I wasn't that great at quick comebacks. I blamed it on the knot of tension in my stomach. "Why don't you pull that stick out of your ass..." I fumbled with the pin on my shirt, hoping he didn't see me as I pricked my finger. "...and whack yourself over the head with it?"

The moment Uriel opened his mouth to respond, I moved and shoved my finger toward his mouth, putting the blood still bubbling up from my finger into his system. I had no reason not to think this would work. There was no precedence that said the angel had to *want* to be corporeal for my blood to work. Still, I knew I was going to be in for a fight once he realized what I had done.

Pulling my finger back just as fast as I had put it into his mouth, I wiped it on the underside of my dress. I'd felt the warm wet of his tongue before removing my finger and knew that the angel in front of me was very much now touchable. Glancing around, I checked to see if anyone had noticed Uriel appearing out of nowhere.

Nope. Too busy sucking face.

"What did you do to me, human?" Uriel practically shouted. I jumped up and covered his mouth with my hand.

"Would you be quiet?"

Uriel shook me off and stared down at his form,

a curious but pissed-off expression on his face. "What have you done to me? I'm... human."

"No, you're not." I rolled my eyes. "You're still you just..." I waved a hand at him. "Visible and very much touchable." I poked him in the side, and a wicked sort of glee came from making him jump at my touch. "So, now, we're on the same level."

"I did not give you permission to make me corporeal." Uriel glowered down at me. "You have tainted me with your human blood."

"Oh, get over it." I waved him off and walked away, tired of his bitching. "Tell me where the guys are, and I'll tell you how to go back to the way you were."

Of course, I didn't mention the fact that he would turn back on his own eventually. There was no need to show all my cards. This was a power play, after all.

I hurried up the steps with Uriel close behind me, still bitching about me violating him. Geez, you'd think I'd raped him or something. I'd never had someone be so ungrateful in my life. I didn't head to Andre's table, happy to see him in a conversation with someone else, but instead headed for the buffet table.

"And another thing, angels are not supposed to

indulge in human temptations," Uriel's bitch fest continued. "It is against our natures and the rules. You are lucky you haven't been smited for your insolence."

Sighing, I picked up a miniature cheese cake and shoved it into his still-griping mouth. His eyes widened and he was forced to chew unless he wanted to choke. I watched with growing interest as his expression changed from horrified to delighted. His eyes searched the table for the thing I had put in his mouth, and I quickly moved out of his way.

"See, not everything is as horrible as you think it is." I smugly watched him pick up more things to try on the table. He almost loved food more than me.

"Where are they?" I tried again while his mouth was full of deviled egg.

"Here, Jane."

Gabriel appeared on the other side of the buffet table a sad expression on his face. Michael and Lucifer appeared next each of them, taking up a place a few feet away from me and not moving to get closer.

"Where did you go?" I asked them, not caring that anyone could be watching me. "And why do you look like someone died?"

"Our apologies, love." Lucifer grimaced. "Several things have happened as of late, and we couldn't get away."

"But you're back now, right?" I shot a look at them all, eager for them to assuage my fears and tell me what I wanted to hear.

"For the moment." Michael nodded. "We have to get back." His eyes moved to Uriel. "We've only come to collect this one and explain."

"Explain what?" I stepped toward them, but they took a step away from me. Frowning, I shook my head. "What's happening? Why won't you let me touch you?"

"Oh, Jane. We want to but we can't." Gabriel's eyes were full of pain and sorrow, so much so that I felt it pang in my heart and tears came to my eyes.

"Why not?" My voice wavered as they exchanged a look. "What you can't even tell me that? I thought you were here to explain?"

"Jane?" Andre took my arm, trying to turn me to him. "What's going on? Why are you yelling at this man?" His eyes widened as he took in Uriel's appearance. "I don't believe I know you."

Uriel scanned over Andre and then sniffed before turning back to the table dismissing him.

"I'm fine," I told Andre, taking a moment to talk

to him. "I just need a moment, okay? I'll come find you later."

Andre's brows furrowed, but he seemed to see how distressed I was and nodded. He left me to go back to his table, but his eyes never left me.

"You should give him a chance, love," Lucifer said in a small voice that made me mad.

"No. I won't give him a chance." I waved my arms in the air as aggravation surged through me. "I have you. I don't need him. Now, just stop all this nonsense and tell me what is going on."

Michael took a step toward me, closer but still not within touching distance. "I wish we could, Jane, but it's better this way. Just trust that we are going to do whatever it takes to keep you safe."

"Keep me safe by being here," I quipped and moved toward him, my hand out reached. They moved back as if I had some kind of disease. They really knew how to hurt a girl.

"I can't do this." Gabriel ran a hand through his hair and met my gaze. "I'm sorry." Then he was gone.

"This is for your own good, pet." Lucifer gave me a half smile, one hand in his pocket. "Just know we will be thinking of you every step of the way."

I gaped at the empty space the Devil once stood

and then to the lone angel still there. "Will you come back?" I didn't try to hide the stutter in my voice, my voice breaking with emotion.

Michael's expression softened. "I won't lie to you. I do not know. We will try everything in our power to come back to you."

"Pinkie promise?" I held my hand out to him which caused him to smile.

Michael's head tilted to the side, and that sad smile on his face killed me. He didn't promise or loop his pinkie with mine. Instead, he grabbed Uriel who tried to grab as many mini cheese cakes as possible with him before they too disappeared.

Wet tracks fell down my face and I vaguely heard Andre talking to me. Asking me something or another but I just didn't care. They were gone. My angels were gone.

22

Taping up the last box, I sighed. We'd been packing for hours and I was getting tired of it. Who knew I could accumulate so much stuff over such a small period of time?

"Are you sure you want to do this?" Mandy sat down another box next to the one I'd just boxed up. "You don't have to close up shop just because your…"

"My primary source of power is gone?" I let out a bitter laugh. "I can't exactly be a psychic detective if I have no psychic powers."

"You were still a good detective." She placed her hand on my shoulder. "You don't need them for that."

"Yes, I do," I murmured.

It wasn't just that I needed their powers. It was more than that. Everything around me at the office reminded me of them. The places we had laughed. Kissed. Made love. Yes, I loved all three of them, and I regret every day that I never told them all just how much.

And now, I may never get to.

Three months. It had been three months since the angels left to save me. Three months since my whole life got turned upside down.

I knew why they did it. I wasn't an idiot, but it didn't make it any easier to swallow. The only way to keep me safe was to leave.

It must have worked because I hadn't seen hide nor hair of Uriel or any other angel since then. Not that I was craving to see that psychopath but the others... well, you don't tell a girl you love them than disappear into thin air without a word. It's just plain rude.

The first few days, I didn't think anything of it. I just went about my days wondering when they were going to make a reappearance. Then when it was clear they weren't coming back any time soon, I got pissed off.

I yelled and screamed at them, at God, at everything. I broke things and ended up in the ER to get stitches and still they didn't come.

Then came the sadness. The grief. I cried and cried until I couldn't breathe, and my chest hurt. Mandy took time off work to be with me. She told me she feared I'd do something crazy, like try to get to Heaven the old-fashioned way.

I laughed at her. If I was going anywhere, it would be to Hell, but at least Lucifer would be there to greet me.

I would love to say I had too much pride to kill myself to get to them, but it wasn't pride. I'd never had much pride to begin with. Hard to when your entire life had been one big joke after another. I was always the butt of somebody's one-liners. No, what stopped me was fear.

A damn coward was what I was. I couldn't take the pills that I had in the bathroom to help me sleep. I couldn't cut my wrists or drink myself to death because I feared that God would punish me for even thinking I had a chance of happiness with them. So, if I did happen to die, he wouldn't even let me see them. I liked to imagine there was a sort of purgatory for people like me. People that don't belong in either place. At least, that was what some religions stated. I wasn't sure what I believed. I just knew I wanted to see them, to get some kind of explanation.

Which was the hardest part. Not knowing. I had no idea where they went or when they were coming back if at all. I didn't know if they ended up in trouble for what happened with Uriel and the others. Or if they just forgot about me.

I sure as hell would have liked to forget about them.

Or at least, I kept telling myself that.

"Jane?"

I jerked my head up, my mind still muddled with thoughts. "What?"

"Did you hear a word I said?" Mandy asked, her hands on her hips, her lips pursed in a frown.

"No, I didn't." I offered her an apologetic smile. "I'm sorry, my head's all..." I wiggled a hand in the air by my head. "What did you say?"

"I asked, if you were going to return Andre's call?" She arched a brow at me. "He's not going to wait forever, you know. And you could do worse than a billionaire who wants nothing but to buy you things."

Even though I had solved Andre's case of the missing golden trophy, he still called me. The day after the guys disappeared, he asked me out on an official date. I'd done the normal thing and beat around the bush about why I couldn't go. Then when the guys never reappeared, I told him I was getting over a break up. Andre's response to that was flowers. Lots of flowers and chocolates. He got points for trying at least, but still, I couldn't bring myself to tell him yes.

"Pfft." I picked up my stapler and sat it back down in the open box on the desk. "He'd be a rebound if anything. I couldn't do that to him."

"Rebound or not, you should go out with him." Mandy bumped my shoulder with her own. "Get out of the house, out of this office. Just live. Do something out of the ordinary and then maybe things will get easier."

"I know." I nodded. "And I'm trying. Why do you think I'm quitting." I stacked another box onto the table and then picked them all up and moved toward the door. "I just want this part of my life to be over."

Mandy followed me out to my car, and we put the boxes in the back seat. "What are you going to do then? Go back to school? You already have a bachelor's and an associate's degree. Maybe you should try and do something with them?"

"Yeah, in religious studies and business. What

am I going to do, open a church?" I scoffed and turned my keys over and over in my hand. I spun the key ring around my finger and then grasped them tight, so tight they bit into my hand. I welcomed the pain though, it helped keep me grounded.

Shrugging, Mandy crossed her arms over her chest. "I don't know, but you gotta do something. You can't just wallow at your parent's house. I'm sure they're getting tired of you already."

"They're my parents," I scoffed. "They love me and support me."

"But they're mostly retired and want alone time without adult children mooching off of them."

"I am not mooching. I have my own money, thank you very much. I just..." I trialed off and turned my head away. "I don't want to be alone."

"Then move in with me." Mandy wrapped her arms around me to pull me into a hug. "My lease is almost up, we should just get an apartment together. Then you won't be alone, and I won't have to cook."

I laughed, but I didn't really feel it. "You mean, I'll order take out because if I am the one doing the cooking, then we're both going to be dead. That stray cat that hovers around your fire escape will sneak in and eat our corpses off the floor. All they'll find of us will be our bones picked clean and a fat cat."

Mandy wrinkled her nose. "Ew. Imagery."

I shook my head. "I'm alright. Thanks though." I took a deep breath and sighed before glancing back at the Gotcha! Sign still painted on the window. "Nah, I'll figure it out. Eventually."

"Alright, well. I have to get back to the precinct. Will you be okay?" She leaned back and looked at my face as if she was searching for any sign that I was going to break.

Pushing her away, I smiled. "Yeah, I'll be fine. Go tell O'Connor I have an aunt that would love to be his sugar mama. Just let me know. I'll get him her number."

Mandy laughed and shook her head before heading back to her car.

I watched her drive away until she was gone. Then I turned back to the office. Now that I was alone, I had to face saying goodbye to this place I'd once loved and the guys. It was a good of place as any to get it over and done with.

Mandy was right. I couldn't hold onto them forever. They were angels. I was human. I only had one life to live, and if I used it waiting for them to come back, then it would be like I never lived at all.

The door chimed as I entered the office. The interior empty and cold without my sparse furnishings to fill it. The desk was the only thing that sat in the middle of the office, and that had come with the place. It didn't seem right to take it even if I'd spent many hours christening it with the guys. I smiled fondly at it and then frowned.

Stop it, Jane. They're gone and they're never coming back. You have to let go. Let them go.

I sighed a long sappy sigh and closed my eyes. I saw this once in a movie. I wanted to start over. Start fresh so I had to give back to the world what it had given to me.

Holding my hands out to my sides, I took a deep breath and as I pushed it out imagined all the hope and love I had for the guys were being blown out of me. I would leave them here with all my happy memories of them. I would go back into the world as a new woman. Reborn. A soft and new as baby's bottom.

Okay, even I knew that was going a bit far.

But all the same. I was done. They were gone. Time to call Andre and move on.

Relaxing, I dropped my hands and opened my eyes. Time to go.

Turning around, I jerked back. My hand going to my chest and my eyes widening. Standing in front of me, after I did all that cleansing and starting over crap were the three pains in the ass angels I'd been trying to get over.

I put my hands on my hips with a scowl. "Where have you been?"

Michael, Gabriel, and Lucifer stood there as glorious and deliciously edible as ever with equally contrite expressions on their faces. Okay, so Lucifer wasn't contrite. He was more amused than anything.

"Sorry, we're late." Gabriel moved closer to me first. "We had to see an all-powerful being about a girl."

"We did not expect it to take so long," Michael added as he followed after Gabriel.

Lucifer shook his head and laughed. "I knew it would. Father is stubborn and wanted to make us work for it." He too circled in around me.

I stared at them in wonder. Wondering how they came back, why they were here now, and if they would leave again. I couldn't do it. I couldn't do it anymore.

"You're too late." I smiled sadly at them. "It's over. We're over. I've moved on."

"Oh?" Michael glanced at the other two, and they exchanged a peculiar look. "Are you now?" He reached out, and I waited for the usual buzzing to start but all I felt was the warmth of his hand on my face.

"What?" I gaped. "You're touching me. How are you touching me?" I grinned and laughed, tears leaking out before I could catch them. I placed my hand on top of his to make sure I wasn't dreaming it. Nope, he was there.

"Now, don't give him all the credit." Lucifer placed his hand on my waist and pulled me toward him. "He's not the only one with a brand new corporeal form, and it has missed you terribly." He wagged his brows at me, making me giggle.

I hugged him close and then kissed him desperately. Pulling away, I looked to Gabriel who had been watching with a small smile on his face. "Are you corporeal now too?"

Gabriel nodded.

"Then what are you waiting for? Come here." I jumped from Lucifer to Gabriel, and wrapped my arms around him tightly, afraid that if I let him go, he'd be gone.

After I'd gotten over the fact that they were here and touchable without my blood, I asked them, "How'd this happen? You are here to stay right?"

Michael embraced me and pressed his mouth to my forehead. "God works in mysterious ways. We are here to keep you safe for as long as you need us."

"Well, then." I chuckled at his explanation. "I think I'll need you for the next sixty or seventy years. I hope you're ready, because I won't be holding back."

The guys surrounding me on all sides peered back at me with equally affectionate looks of love. Just like that, my life had been turned upside down once again by three totally hot and hard to handle angels.

And I couldn't be happier.

THANK YOU FOR READING!

Thanks for joining me on this journey.
I hope you all enjoyed Michael, Lucifer, and
Gabriel as much as I did

AUTHOR'S NOTE

Come hang out with me in my Reader's Group on Facebook!

Find out all about my works, sneak peeks of works in progress, and exclusive giveaways.

Don't want to interact but want to be on the up and up?

Follow me on Social Media

Facebook.com/erinrbedford

@erin_bedford

Want to be the first to know about my new releases?

Erinbedford.com/newsletter